LUCIFER

LUCIFER

Alexander Kosoris

IGUANA

Published by Iguana Books
720 Bathurst Street, Suite 303
Toronto, Ontario, Canada
M5V 2R4

Publisher: Greg Ioannou
Editor: Andrea Douglas
Front cover design: Jane Awde Goodwin
Book layout design: Kate Unrau

Library and Archives Canada Cataloguing in Publication

Kosoris, Alexander, 1986-, author
Lucifer / Alexander Kosoris.

Issued in print and electronic formats.
ISBN 978-1-77180-063-1 (pbk.). ISBN 978-1-77180-064-8 (epub).
ISBN 978-1-77180-065-5 (kindle). ISBN 978-1-77180-066-2 (pdf).

I. Title.

PS8621.O85L82 2014 C813'.6 C2014-904208-6
C2014-904209-4

This is an original print edition of *Lucifer*.

To my darling wife, Tabitha.

Without her constant encouragement and assessment, this novel would only be an empty shell of its current self.

Chapter 1

In the Beginning

God sat comfortably in His high-backed leather swivel chair. The week had been pretty hectic overall, but this morning was uncharacteristically slow. He really looked forward to Sunday; a Saturday at this pace was the perfect thing to ease Him into the day of rest. It was almost noon, and He could already vividly taste the flavors intermingling in His pastrami-on-rye sandwich that was waiting for lunch to see Him again. Of course, He didn't have to eat, but He liked the taste.

God casually glanced out the window. His office was located at the top of a ninety-six-storey building. God enjoyed watching through His large window, observing not only the majestic view of all the heavens but also the angels bustling around, to and fro, at a steady pace far below: rush, rush, rush. How small they appeared from His vantage point; they looked like humans from up there.

He directed His attention back to the inside of His office. His large oak desk was barren, aside from the pen and pad near the corner. The two chairs on the opposite side were plain black. All along one wall were dark gray filing cabinets. He had thought about making the operation computerized, to reduce all the files that He needed to keep, but He was having a hard time finding the time, or at least that was what He told anyone who asked. The truth of the matter was He didn't really care; the old system had worked this long, anyway, so no harm done. Two ferns graced His office with their presence, one near the door and the other by the window, taking some of the excess carbon dioxide and turning it into oxygen. He, of course, didn't need to breathe, but He liked having the plants around.

The only decoration God had in His office was a small painting on the wall between the two ferns. The painting was called *Impression, Sunrise*, and it was painted by Claude Monet, made especially for Him. He enjoyed the way the warm colors mixed with the overall coolness of the painting. As much as God liked the painting, however, He knew that He probably would have enjoyed having a neo-cubist piece taking up the wall in place of the Monet, but that wouldn't have worked. He couldn't have something loud and obscure on His wall. What would people think? This was a place of business.

There was a quiet knock on His door, which was open. God looked upon His guest with a friendly face, as to somewhat abate his timid nature. "Come in, Lucifer. Have a seat," God said, motioning to one of the chairs.

In walked Lucifer. He sat exactly where he was directed to sit. Lucifer was an angel of average height with a slender build and red hair. His skin was quite pale, and his eyes constantly displayed a look of uneasiness that he could not hide when he found himself in situations that were uncomfortable for him, which were most of them. He seemed out of place no matter his setting, but especially so within God's office. Lucifer tried to make himself as small as possible, so as not to anger God in any way.

There they sat in silence for a moment. Omniscient as He was, God took the time to observe Lucifer without looking directly at him, witnessing the growing anxiety Lucifer was experiencing with each lapsing second. While, in actuality, hardly any time had passed, the quiet seemed to last an eternity for Lucifer. Lucifer knew not what to say or do, and fidgeted awkwardly as he waited for something to end the stillness. Eventually, God did.

"I'm sure you're wondering why I've requested you to come to My office today."

Lucifer looked up at Him, replying, "Yes. Yes, I was curious. I don't normally come up here that often." He then paused, carefully considering what he said. "Come to think of it, I haven't ever been up here."

"I have a favor to ask of you," added God, ignoring Lucifer's comment. "I need you to do something for Me."

"Of course," Lucifer quickly replied.

"Lucifer, how do you feel about your job?"

He thought about it and chose his words very cautiously, "Oh, I like my job. It's a fine job."

"But do you really like it?" God asked, looking at him quizzically.

Lucifer tried to see where He was going with this. They both knew that there was no point in hiding anything. "Why do You ask?"

"Oh, I just wanted to know before I broke the news to you. I have big plans for you, Lucifer."

Lucifer's eyes lit up. "Oh, yeah?"

Now donning a large smile, God continued, "Yes. I have a new position for you. Very important, and you're the only one for the job."

"What is the job?" Lucifer's curiosity was growing.

"Well, let's just say that you'll be..." God paused, appearing to be finding the correct choice of words. "Testing people."

Lucifer pondered this for only a second. He became excited at the thought of a promotion, and he didn't attempt to hide this. "Okay, I'll do it," he responded.

"Hold on a second." God leaned forward, the pleasantness in His voice almost completely gone in an instant. "It's not that simple. I mean, I can't just move you from your current position over to this one. I don't want to play favorites or anything, and I'm sure there are a lot of others who want this job, too."

"Well, what do You have to do?"

God paused again for emphasis. He continued what He was saying, placing His hand on His chest as He did so, "It's not what I have to do." He moved His hand from His chest and used it to motion toward Lucifer, finishing His thought, "It's what you have to do."

"Well, what do I have to do?" Lucifer asked immediately.

"Rebel," God answered simply.

Lucifer said nothing, waiting for the Lord to finish His thought, but He said nothing more. Lucifer eventually asked, "What exactly do You mean?"

"I mean exactly what I said." God paused again before adding, "Rebel ... against Me."

Lucifer grew more confused. "But, how would I be rebelling if You are telling me to do it?"

"Don't ask; just do it."

"Okay."

They sat in silence once more. Lucifer fidgeted, wanting to get more information out of the Lord. Eventually, he spoke, "But..."

"What is it?" inquired God, clasping His hands together and resting His chin upon them.

"But You know everything, right?"

"Right."

"And You can see everything." Lucifer hesitated once more before adding, "Right?"

"Right."

"Then how can I rebel?"

"Don't ask. Just figure it out."

"Okay." Lucifer paused again, his mind befuddled. Grasping at straws, Lucifer asked, "When should I do this?"

"Surprise Me," God said.

Lucifer stepped out of God's office and made his way to the elevator. He passed by the large desk immediately outside the office and casually took a peek at God's secretary. He couldn't believe his eyes; she was simply stunning! She, of course, did not look up at him, being far too engrossed in her crossword puzzle. He regarded her closely, slowing his pace to allow himself a better look. Her simple white blouse was hardly able to conceal the form of her exquisite bosom. Lucifer extended his neck in order to observe her magnificent form completely, seeing a black skirt that was so short that it didn't really appear to be serving much of a purpose. Had her legs not been crossed, he most definitely would have had a clear view of the wonders below. Lucifer could feel a passion growing inside him; lust overcame him entirely, and he felt urges the likes of which were completely foreign to him.

Wait! No! Stop! he thought to himself, only now remembering that God could hear his every thought. *I'm not looking at her. There, I stopped. It's okay, she's out of my league anyway.*

He pressed the Down button, causing it to light up. The elevator was taking its sweet time; with thoughts of being monitored by God, Lucifer's wait seemed horrendously long.

He kept his eyes on the elevator door. *Come on, come on,* he thought. *Not that I'm really in a hurry ... or that uncomfortable. I just want to get back ... to work. I wonder if pressing the button again will help speed it up. I'm sure it couldn't hurt; maybe it didn't register the first time.*

He pressed the button again; nothing changed. He glanced back at the secretary. *No! Eyes forward! Don't think about her breasts. I mean thighs. I mean—*

Ding! The sound of the doors opening was music to his ears. Lucifer hit the number fourteen, corresponding to the number of the floor on which he worked, and then tapped on the Door Close button repeatedly. When the doors finally obeyed his command, Lucifer breathed a sigh of relief. It was as though the box that enclosed him somehow helped to conceal his thoughts and actions from a certain individual upstairs. Lucifer knew better deep down, but he still took some solace in his refuge of self-deception.

Lucifer hardly had a moment to bask in the wonderful loneliness of the elevator when it jerked to a stop. Ding! The doors opened, and in walked two other angels, both walking with their respective suit jackets slung over one shoulder, exposing their identical black suspenders. One carried himself with an air of importance, no doubt cultivated through years of always being right. No one could really fault him for that belief; the angels around him supported it. But no one could really fault any of them, either, as it was hard to argue with someone when fact and reason are foregone in lieu of charm and persistence. The simulated success of this angel resulted in the admiration of many angels within the office, looking to translate his shining example into some success of their own.

Lucifer knew this angel simply as Nathaniel from the Marketing department. They had met before, but Lucifer never seemed to leave a memorable impression in Nathaniel's mind, which led to several introductions between the two of them. Lucifer looked forward as the other angel hit the button for the ground floor. The two intruders continued their conversation.

"So, long story short, I got a meeting with Michael," explained Nathaniel, Michael being the manager of Marketing, "and he tells me that he's interested in what I have to say, but he has to meet in half an hour. Naturally, I'm scrambling to get my act in gear and make something at least resembling a pitch."

"Oh man," the other angel responded with genuine interest. The excited look upon his face suggested he was enthralled with every word that came out of Nathaniel's mouth. "That's just brutal."

"Tell me about it," Nathaniel continued. "Anyway, my pitch goes well, as usual. Now I just have to get some angels from other departments in on it and go from there. You know, cast out the line and see what's biting, so to speak."

They both laughed big. As the laugh subsided, they looked away from each other, only now scanning their surroundings. Nathaniel smiled to himself, content with the effect his anecdote had on the other angel, and caught a glimpse of Lucifer out of the corner of his eye. Deciding it would be unfortunate to waste his charms standing in the elevator silently, Nathaniel turned his whole body toward Lucifer in order to continue using his amazing interpersonal skills to their fullest potential.

"Say, you look familiar," he said to Lucifer. "What department are you with?"

Lucifer responded simply, "Research and Development."

"R&D, R&D..." Nathaniel was looking up at the ceiling, tapping his forehead as he tried extremely hard to recall the information. "You look so familiar. Have we met before?"

"Probably at some point or another. My—"

"Wait, don't tell me," Nathaniel cut him off. "Your name's ... Lester? Leonard?"

At least he remembered how it started. Lucifer corrected him, "Lucifer, actually—"

"Lucifer!" he sounded more excited. "That's what I was about to say! Lucy, baby, how have you been?"

"Okay, I guess. I—"

"Great," he interrupted, slapping Lucifer's arm. At Nathaniel's firm touch, Lucifer jumped. "Say, would you be able to help me out? I was talking with Michael, one of the big boys, about some of that science stuff humans are going to have. We want to explain some things in that Bible book we're working on, kind of ... 'instructions,'" Nathaniel said, making finger quotes, "so to say, and I was hoping we could make sure we don't have any discrepancies when human science improves. That's where I was hoping I could get someone from R&D to help out. So how about it, Lucy, baby? It *is* a team effort."

Lucifer just wanted this conversation to end. He thought about what was said for a moment, and then shakily told Nathaniel, "Personally, I'm working on human personality right now, so I don't know too much about it. I — I don't know who I'd talk to about this, but I guess I can try passing it on to someone working on carbon dating or ... fossils ... or something."

Ding! The elevator doors opened on Lucifer's floor, and he started to exit. "Here, just give them my card," Nathaniel said, handing it to him. As the doors were closing, he continued with a huge smile on his face, "Take it easy, but not too easy. Am I right?"

Lucifer stood staring at the elevator door for a moment, reflecting on the exchange he just had. He found it interesting that Nathaniel wanted to shape the research findings to conform to his book, when it made logical sense to Lucifer to do things the other way around. He thought about ripping up Nathaniel's card and discarding it, but he merely stared at it. *I suppose I can hand it off to someone if I get a chance,* he thought. *Really, what's the harm?* He put the card in his pocket and then continued to his office, which was just around the corner.

"Oh, crap, am I late again?"

The angel who spoke was Raphael. He and Lucifer shared an office, and Lucifer couldn't think of a better angel to work with in a confined space. Maybe it was because they had worked together for such a long time, but Raphael was the only angel that Lucifer truly felt comfortable around.

Lucifer did not respond. After looking at the clock, Raphael added, "No, I'm right on time. Hey, did God make you work right through lunch?"

Lucifer looked up from his work, smiling, "He didn't *make* me."

"I guess I see why you're the one getting summoned upstairs," Raphael said with a laugh. "Speaking of which, how'd that go? Are you going to leave me behind in the world of business?"

"As a matter of fact, I may. While you were out—" Lucifer stopped what he was saying to look Raphael up and down "—buying new suits, I was making something of myself." He did a double take. "Say, that is a new suit. What's the occasion?"

"Oh, you like it?" Raphael asked, twirling to show off his new pinstriped three-piece suit. "Yeah, I've been eyeing this baby up for a little while now, so I finally bit the bullet and got it," he flung his suit jacket onto the coat rack, sat down, and swiveled around in his chair. He performed a complete revolution, bringing his feet down in time to end the spin facing Lucifer, saying, "Just in time for my meeting with Marketing, I might add."

Raphael knocked on his desk once. Lucifer looked surprised, saying, "That's right, I forgot about it. You seem ... enthusiastic. It must have gone well."

"Actually, I don't think it's possible for a meeting with the angels from Marketing to go well," Raphael replied. "They're all such ... how should I put it?" He thought hard about the correct choice of words, eventually saying, "Ah! Pompous bores."

Lucifer laughed. Raphael continued, bobbing as he spoke, "It's always a song and dance about making life on Earth perfect and making Heaven look even sweeter and making them look good to the higher-ups and blah, blah, blah. I don't have time to hear about that; I've got my plate full designing the landscapes of Western Canada."

"Well, if it didn't go well, why so energetic?"

"Oh," Raphael knocked on the desk twice more, "free coffee."

Lucifer laughed again, and Raphael added, "And, as you may or may not know about me, I hardly drink coffee, so just having a bit gets me very wired."

They sat briefly without speaking, but Raphael broke the silence by pulling out his blueprints. They had been working quietly for a few minutes when they were interrupted by a knock on their open door. Both looked up to see Gabriel, the manager of the Research and Development department.

Gabriel was somewhat of an oddity. To a stranger, he appeared quite intimidating, being arguably the largest angel the heavens produced, due in part to the large size God blessed him with and also the long hours he spent in the gym. However, anyone who knew him was aware that he was also arguably the friendliest angel in the office.

"Hi guys," he said softly, "how's everything going?"

"Great, Gabe," Raphael responded immediately.

Lucifer nodded in agreement. Gabriel smiled, adding, "Do either of you need anything?"

They both thought about it and shook their heads.

He continued, "No supplies?"

Lucifer said, "I don't think so."

Gabriel looked back to Raphael, asking, "Need to book any testing rooms?"

Raphael answered, "Not at this time."

Gabriel looked to Lucifer, and back to Raphael. He finally asked, "Want some coffee?"

Both Lucifer and Raphael smiled. Raphael added, "Actually, I think we're alright, Gabe. Thanks, though."

Finally satisfied with the status quo, Gabriel nodded, saying, "Okay, then. Keep up the good work."

He then left, and they returned to their projects. This was what the angels in the department came to expect of Gabriel: He was around and made himself accessible, but he was never breathing down your neck to get results. As such, Lucifer and Raphael were always quite happy having him drop by.

Raphael looked up from his blueprints, asking, "Oh, drinks tonight? I would say I'm buying, but I just spent all my money on a new suit."

Lucifer didn't have to take the time to think about it. "Oh sure, I could use a night out," he replied.

They continued to work briefly. Suddenly, Lucifer hesitated. "Actually, could I take a rain check?" he said. "I didn't really get a timeline, but I have a lot to do right now."

"Are you talking about...?" Raphael motioned upward with his thumb; Lucifer nodded.

"I suppose I understand," Raphael continued.

They quietly went on with their work. Raphael sat drawing slowly and meticulously, while Lucifer wrote some notes. Only a few minutes passed when Raphael broke the silence once more. "We won't be out too late. And, really, even if we are out a bit late, you still have Sunday to do whatever you need to..."

LUCIFER

Lucifer audibly put down his pen and stared at Raphael. After delivering his unwavering, stony glare for some time, Lucifer eventually said, "If I say yes, will you let me get back to work?"

"You bet."

Chapter 2

The Pearly Gates

Whenever Lucifer and Raphael went out drinking, they frequented a quiet little pub on the trendy side of Heaven called the Pearly Gates. It really was a miracle that so few angels drank there. Peter, the owner and bartender, always managed to get the best musical talents Heaven had to offer to come and play in the bar. The Pearly Gates also had a quaint atmosphere and arguably the best beer in Heaven. Some angels would insist that Cloud Nine, just five blocks away, was superior, what with its large selection of lagers. However, Lucifer's and Raphael's sophisticated palates delighted at Peter's interesting concoctions, from weissbier to stouts, brewed right there in the back.

On this particular night, Peter had a pianist sitting on the small stage in the center of the room playing some light jazzy music. The pub was constructed to deliver amazing acoustics, and tables were laid out all around the stage to allow each patron an unobstructed view of the performer. This was quite fortuitous for both Lucifer and Raphael, as they both were entranced by her. Raphael loved watching how her fingers glided effortlessly over the keys, producing the masterful sounds that flowed to his ears; he took in the melodious tunes while contently sipping his drink. Lucifer, however, was more preoccupied with the look of the angel herself; he regarded her curly blonde locks quivering as she moved her voluptuous form. Her long gown flowed around her, a slit in the side revealing her silken leg, almost as though it was peeking out merely to tease him. Lucifer was unable to control the widening of his pupils as he regarded her elegant movements.

She finished playing and sat for a moment, awaiting applause. Light applause was delivered by the few patrons. She got up and slowly made her way over to the bar. The other angels went back to their conversations, and Lucifer watched her walk, carefully shifting her weight over from one leg to the other, showing off her shapely rear. Taking her seat, she ordered a drink. Lucifer continued his stare, observing every little movement she made as she casually flicked her hair over her shoulder and reached into her purse, shrugging her shoulders slightly as she did so. Out of her purse came lipstick; she slowly twisted the bottom and brought it to her lips, firmly spreading it along the bottom lip and curling her lips in, rubbing them together to give a perfectly even coat. She then brought her glass to her mouth and sipped her drink deliberately, bringing her tongue across her top lip afterwards.

"Lucifer?" With that, Lucifer realized Raphael had been trying to get his attention for some time already. Raphael chuckled to himself, adding, "I really think you work too hard. I mean, look at you, off daydreaming."

"No, no," Lucifer responded quickly. "It's not that, it's just..." Lucifer hesitated. After some quick deliberation, he said, "Anyway, weren't you going to tell me about your date with...?"

Raphael's eyes widened. He finished Lucifer's thought for him. "Who, Abigail?"

Lucifer nodded approvingly.

"I don't know," continued Raphael, "what's there to tell? I had a great time, and she seemed to as well. We saw that new musical that has been getting all those rave reviews."

Lucifer thought hard about it. "Oh yeah, I heard about that one ... *Harps*?"

"Yes," said Raphael. "I enjoyed it, although it wasn't as good as *Wings of the Steed*. But that's not important. Abby's been great; I really like being around her, and she really has some ... insightful things to talk about." He paused, smiling as he stared off, fondly remembering his time with her. Snapping out of his trance, he looked back at Lucifer, asking, "What about you? Have you started seeing anyone?"

Lucifer looked up at Raphael, then quickly back down to his drink, responding simply, "No."

They sat in silence. Raphael added, "I don't think I can even remember you being with anyone."

Lucifer looked back at him. "I can't remember the last time I was out on a date, either," he said, swishing his drink around as he spoke. "I guess I've just been too busy with work to think about that very much."

"I don't know," said Raphael. "There must be more to it than that. Are you just not interested in dating right now?" He stopped for a moment before adding, "Because there's nothing wrong with that."

Lucifer considered what he said. "No, it's not that. I guess if the right angel came along ... I suppose I just don't have enough opportunities to meet anyone ... interesting."

Raphael raised his free hand up a bit and looked back and forth, then back to Lucifer, saying, "Well, we're out right now. I know we're not really out to meet anyone, but if you see someone you like, you just have to let go of your inhibitions and talk with her." He carefully looked around the room, continuing, "What about any of them?"

Raphael pointed at a group of three angels several tables over from them. Lucifer immediately grabbed his arm, bringing it back down. He said, "Careful — they'll see you."

Raphael merely smiled. He raised his eyebrows, saying, "Well?"

Lucifer looked over, and then back at Raphael. "I don't know..."

"Come on. You must think at least one of them is cute."

Lucifer thought they were all cute. "I just ... What would I even say?"

"Don't think too much about it. You just have to go and do it," Raphael responded excitedly. "Just walk on over and introduce yourself. Really, what's the worst thing that could happen?"

Lucifer thought about that. "I don't know ... I get rejected."

This egged Raphael on. "So? *If* you get rejected, you don't know them and you probably won't ever see them again."

"What do you mean?" asked Lucifer, irritation resonating in his voice. "For all we know, they're regulars here. They'll probably be here next time we're around."

"But who cares?" Raphael said. "Even if they reject you, they'll probably find the fact that you're interested very ... flattering."

Lucifer turned and looked at them again. He thought about it for some time before replying, "I don't think I can do it."

He hesitated once again. Still looking toward the group, he added, "I mean, there's three of them."

"Okay, okay, how about her?" Picking up his drink, Raphael waved it in the general vicinity of the pianist before taking another sip.

Lucifer looked back at him, his eyes widening. He let out an exasperated laugh and said, "Yeah, okay. I'll just go over there and talk to her right now." He followed that statement up with a large gulp of his own drink.

Raphael waited for him to put his glass back down before continuing, "Why not? I saw the way you were looking at her."

Just then, Peter came to clear some glasses off of their table. Lucifer looked back at the pianist. He sighed, "She's way out of my league."

"You see? You see?" Raphael said enthusiastically. "That's your problem. You don't know how much you have to offer."

Lucifer gave another awkward laugh, "Yeah, whatever."

"Yeah, you're too modest," Raphael continued. He looked up at Peter, "Isn't that his problem, Pete?" Lucifer looked up at him as well.

"Sure," Peter said. "You think about it too much. Once you leave your fear behind and realize what you got, you could have 'em eating out of the palm of your hand." Peter looked Lucifer up and down. "You don't even have to do too much. You're a good lookin' guy; your big problem is confidence." He banged the table lightly, emphasizing the word. "Look and sound confident, and I'll bet you could have anyone you want – including my piano-playing friend over there."

All at once, they returned their gazes to the pianist.

Peter added, "If that's what floats your boat."

With that, Peter walked away. Lucifer just continued watching her longingly and sighed.

Chapter 3

Human Interaction

"Lights on."

The lights in the middle of the large room turned on, followed by the lights next to them. The rest began to light up faster and faster until the room was completely illuminated. Lucifer and another angel stood near the middle of the room, which was completely white, except for a small window near the ceiling close to the center of the room.

Lucifer held a clipboard, upon which he was vigorously writing. He stopped for a moment to ask the other angel, "Okay, so what are we doing here today?"

"Well, um, I created a simulation situation for our human models to hopefully ... successfully interact," the angel answered. Feeling his glasses slipping down his nose, the angel also took this opportunity to push them back up to their proper resting place.

"Sounds good. Let's see what they can do." Lucifer then spoke up, "Bring in models."

Two male humans appeared in front of them, completely motionless. They both wore brown slacks along with matching blue sweater vests, and their hair was impeccable. The only real distinguishing characteristic between the two of them, apart from the colors of their hair, was the large black number one on the blond human's chest and the corresponding number two on the chest of the human with the brown hair. Both numbers appeared to be spray-painted on. The four of them stood in silence until Lucifer cleared his throat.

"Oh, yes," the other angel responded. He then shouted, "Run program S-G dot seven!"

Immediately, the two humans' eyes opened. They both turned their bodies slowly toward each other, one taking short steps as he pivoted. Once eye contact was made, they both bounced slightly upon recognition.

"Oh, hello, my friend. You are looking well today," said Human #1.

"Why, thank you. You are looking well, as well," replied Human #2.

"Shall we walk as we continue to have this conversation?" asked #1.

"I find the idea unobjectionable," #2 responded.

They started to pivot their bodies until they faced away from the two angels, and then they began to walk. Lucifer moved beside #1 and stayed next to him. He watched their stiff motions as they took their first steps; they started slowly, but quickened their pace slightly as they went. Human #1 was a bit bouncy in his step; he raised his knees up high as he walked and seemed to have his elbows permanently bent as he swayed them back and forth. Human #2, on the other hand, looked as though he had a hard time bending his knees; he walked with his legs fully extended. It was already an odd sight for Lucifer, but the fact that #2 also kept his arms hanging motionless at his sides made the walk look even stranger.

They continued their conversation as they walked.

"How are you finding your place of business?" asked #2.

"You mean my *job*?" clarified #1.

They stopped in their tracks. Both humans bent their arms and pivoted them so that their hands were on their bellies, and they each went, "Ho, ho, ho," simultaneously, shrugging their shoulders and bouncing as they gave the chuckle. They then continued on their walk.

#1 said, "I am finding it to be an acceptable place of employment." He then stopped and pointed into the air, as though he had had a thought, although Lucifer was skeptical of that. #2 stopped walking as well, and both humans turned their bodies slowly to face each other once more.

"Well, what have we here?" #1 asked, as he reached into his pocket. "It appears as though I am holding on to an apple."

Sure enough, he pulled out an apple for all to see. Lucifer watched in horror as something appeared to be happening to Human #2. He could see the model's face slowly shifting. His eyebrows moved up and down, and his face contorted this way and that. It took some time, but he eventually changed his expression to that of a large smile, as Human #1 waited patiently all the while. Human #2 then responded, "I am seeing that there is an apple in your hand."

"As a token of gratitude for our friendship," #1 added, shifting his body slightly, "I would like to present this apple to you, as a gift."

#1 then proceeded to straighten out his elbow and move his arm forward, holding the apple out for #2 to receive. #2 bent his arm up so that his hand was in front of his face. He then rotated his forearm so his palm was facing away from himself. He straightened his arm in an attempt to grab the apple. Missing, he bent it, repositioned, and tried again. Missing again, he followed suit, bending it, repositioning, and trying once more. He succeeded this time, bringing the apple up and rotating his forearm back so that the apple was immediately in front of his face.

"The gift has been successfully received," #2 said, still with a large grin.

With that, both humans went motionless. Lucifer stood there, speechless.

Nothing was said for a moment, then the other angel pushed his glasses back up his nose, asking, "Well?"

Lucifer looked at him, then back at the humans. Human #1's arm was still extended, and #2 was almost touching his own nose with the apple. He looked down to his notes. Amongst the numerous things written about the robotic quality of their awkward walk and the unnatural patterns of speech, he seemed to be able to focus only on the last thing that was written: *I guess the third time's a charm.*

Seeing that the other angel was waiting for him to say something, anything at all, Lucifer eventually said, "Yes..."

He paused for a few more seconds, adding, "That was definitely an interaction."

They stood in silence again. Not satisfied, the angel tried to get Lucifer to elaborate. "So ... did you like it?"

Lucifer took a moment to carefully consider what he said. He was well aware of how hard the angel had been working on this project, and he didn't want to hurt his feelings. He finally answered, "I didn't *dislike* the interaction."

With that, the angel looked less concerned. The worry transferred to Lucifer's face; he couldn't let this angel go on obliviously with these two walking disasters. He added, "Of course, the interaction was a bit unnatural."

The angel's face turned back to a frown. He began to speak, but Lucifer put up his hand and quickly continued, "Which isn't a bad thing. No, no, it made the interaction much more ... interesting. Maybe *unnatural* wasn't the best description," Lucifer lied. He paused once more, looking for a less judgmental word. "*Novel* may be a better way to describe the interaction," he added.

Seemingly content again, the angel asked, "What would you say was the main strength of the exchange?"

Lucifer was unprepared for that. "Well ... you know, it's hard to say. There were so many ... positive things going on that it would be hard for me to pinpoint one specific ... aspect that rises above the rest."

He could see that the angel was confused. He went on, scratching the top of his scalp as he did so. "But ... if pressed ... I'd say the strength was in the ... *clarity* of the interaction." He paused, considering how he could make more sense of the previous statement. "I was never confused as to what was going on; they both clearly stated that. As well, their actions and gestures were ... expressive." He paused once more before adding, "*Very* expressive ... which isn't to say that it couldn't use improvement."

A look of concern crept to the angel's face. Lucifer quickly said, "But, really, what *doesn't* need improvement? At this stage of research, I would be surprised if the models were behaving exactly the way we wanted them to. No, if you ask me, we're at a ... *reasonable* stage here."

That seemed to satisfy the angel. "If you had to improve something, what would it be?" he asked.

Lucifer was at a loss for words. "I..." He trailed off. "You see, what..."

The angel looked confused again. Lucifer scratched his head again as he glanced over his notes for something constructive to say other than "all of it." He continued, not looking the angel in the eye, "What I think ... is..."

He looked back up at the angel, who eagerly waited for his input. Lucifer quickly spoke, "I think it's too soon after the interaction to really say. I mean, I made plenty of notes, so if you give me a few days to go through them and really ...

consider where to go from here, I can get back to you and give you something you can really use. How does that sound?"

"That sounds reasonable," the angel answered.

Lucifer stood there nodding silently for a moment. The angel joined in, and they continued nodding for a short amount of time. Eventually, they stopped moving their heads. Neither angel knowing how to end the awkwardness, they both turned toward the exit. Lucifer said, "Remove models."

With that, both humans faded away. As the two angels left the empty spot that used to contain the humans, Lucifer said, "Lights off."

The other angel opened the door, and they both stepped out of the room, the lights gradually turning off in sequence as they did so.

Chapter 4

Getting Down to Business

Lucifer worked very hard all week without really considering his special project for God. By Thursday, he felt he should probably attempt something at least resembling rebelling. He spent most of the evening muddling it over in his mind, but he eventually decided to tread the water lightly and do something small that would get angels noticing without getting him in any major trouble.

Friday morning came along, and Lucifer put his plan into action. He spurned his normal business clothes in favor of jeans and a sweater. *Ha,* he thought, *wait until everyone sees me in my casual clothes. This will be sure to cause a mild scandal; these aren't even* business *casual.*

He walked defiantly up to the office building with his head held high. Stopping in front of the main doors, he took a deep breath. *Okay, here goes,* Lucifer thought.

He opened the doors and wandered into the lobby. Passing the angel at the front desk, Lucifer decided to bring the scandal to his attention. He smiled, his eyebrows uncontrollably flickering with excitement, and he said, "Good morning."

The angel looked up and responded, "Good morning."

This was followed by a brief smile of his own, after which he looked back down. Lucifer found himself a bit disappointed that there was no awkward reaction, but no matter. There was plenty of time for others to appreciate the scandalous nature of his attire.

He walked forward to the main elevator, where his jaw practically fell to the floor. There was an angel in front of him reading the newspaper while she waited for the elevator *wearing jeans*. He couldn't believe his eyes. *How can this be?* he thought. *Why in Heaven would someone else decide to wear jeans today?*

Ding! The elevator doors opened, and they both stepped inside. The angel pressed the button for her floor, and she looked up at Lucifer. He stared at her for a moment, still puzzling over the scandalous nature of *her* attire. When he realized what she was waiting for, he finally said, "Oh, uh ... number fourteen."

A small smile crept to her face, and she pressed the button. The doors were beginning to close when someone's hand reached between them. They opened again, revealing another angel in jeans and a plain dark T-shirt. Lucifer was dumbfounded. The angel pressed a button and stood on the other side of Lucifer.

The doors of the elevator closed, and the two angels stood in silence, one reading her paper, the other looking forward, sipping his coffee, and Lucifer looking from one to the other uneasily. The angel reading her paper looked up at one point, feeling someone's eyes watching her; sure enough, Lucifer was looking, rubbing his hands and slightly swaying back and forth. Seeing her make eye contact, Lucifer looked to the floor immediately, then up to the ceiling, and then the floor again.

An insecure smile reached her face once more, and she went back to her paper, trying to ignore whatever was transpiring beside her.

Ding! The elevator doors opened, and a fidgety Lucifer stepped out onto his floor. He was immediately passed by an angel wearing jeans and a short-sleeved collared shirt with a bright floral print and writing on a clipboard as he walked. Lucifer quickly made his way to his office.

He sat at his desk, still rubbing his hands, staring at the door. Several minutes passed, and then in walked Raphael in jeans and a polo shirt, carrying a briefcase. "Good morn—"

"This is some kind of joke, right?" Lucifer interrupted.

Confused, Raphael stopped in his tracks. He looked behind, then back to Lucifer, eventually responding, "What do you mean?"

"What is going on today?" Lucifer said much more loudly, standing back up.

Raphael just stood silently in the doorway for a moment. Having considered it further, he still couldn't make heads or tails of Lucifer's line of questioning. "Um ... what are you talking about?"

Lucifer paused. He was frustrated, and it came across noticeably in his voice, "Everyone's wearing jeans!"

With no response from Raphael, Lucifer shouted, "Why is everyone wearing jeans today?"

Raphael's confusion grew. He carefully said, "Aren't ... you ... wearing jeans?"

Lucifer looked down at his jeans, then back up to Raphael. Frustrated still, he responded, "What does that have to do with anything?"

"Take it easy," Raphael replied, raising his hands in front of him with his palms out, facing Lucifer. "I'm just saying: If you're wearing jeans, why are you so confused that everyone else is?"

"Just humor me for a second," continued Lucifer. "Why is everyone wearing jeans today?"

Looking unsettled, Raphael placed his briefcase on his desk, then wandered slowly to the corkboard on the far wall. He pulled out a tack and removed a sheet of paper. He came back toward Lucifer, cautiously handing him the paper. Dated yesterday, it read:

AS A TOKEN OF EMPLOYEE APPRECIATION, FRIDAYS WILL BE CASUAL DAY AT THE OFFICE, STARTING TOMORROW. SO LEAVE YOUR TIES BEHIND, AND WEAR YOUR JEANS AND T-SHIRTS. HOWEVER, PLEASE DO NOT WEAR ANYTHING THAT OTHER EMPLOYEES MAY FIND INAPPROPRIATE OR OFFENSIVE. ANY COMPLAINTS ABOUT ATTIRE CAN BE BROUGHT TO THE ATTENTION OF YOUR DEPARTMENT MANAGER.

Ding! The elevator doors opened, and out stepped Lucifer. He walked past God's secretary, who didn't seem to notice him once again, and approached the open door to God's office. Looking inside, he could see God beckoning to him.

"Lucifer," God said with a cheerful demeanor. "Come in, come in. What can I do for you?"

Lucifer said nothing and entered the office.

"Come, sit," God added, His hand motioning to a chair.

Lucifer didn't move. He stood there, looking at God, and then at the chair, and back again. Eventually, he reluctantly sat down, a frown on his face. They both were silent, Lucifer thinking of the right words to use, and God waiting patiently for him to use them. Finally, Lucifer asked, "What was that all about?"

God's cheerful expression changed to a look of confusion. He leaned back in His chair and asked, "What seems to be the trouble?"

Lucifer sat in silence for another moment. He then added, "The dress-down day."

God merely sat and said nothing.

Lucifer continued, more annoyance in his voice, "Casual Fridays. You know."

"What do you want Me to tell you, Lucifer?"

"Wearing casual clothes was my act of rebellion," Lucifer said. With God not responding, he added, "I was *rebelling* against You through my choice of wardrobe, going against the established business wear."

God spoke, "Well, it's unfortunate, then, that your first attempt at rebellion coincided with the very first dress-down day." He paused momentarily. Seeing that this was not the answer Lucifer was looking for, He went on, "I felt it would make the angels, My employees, more ... comfortable to work in casual clothes, that's all. I sent the memo out yesterday, and it's too bad that you didn't see it, but we can't turn back the clock now, can we?"

Lucifer opened his mouth to continue the conversation, but he thought better of it and stopped himself. God leaned forward slightly, waiting for Lucifer to continue. He said, "Lucifer, you can speak freely. There are no secrets here anyway."

Lucifer still didn't say anything.

God continued, "Let Me start you off: 'But...'" He paused. Lucifer still sat in silence. God added, "'...You...'" There was another pause, with no response. God said quickly, "'...knew I was going to try rebelling this way?'"

Lucifer finally piped up, pointing at God as he spoke, "Yeah, You *knew* I was not going to follow the dress code, even though You sent the memos out yesterday. And ... and, *knowing* what I know, You sent out those memos ... *preemptively*, knowing that it was going to happen. How am I supposed to rebel against You if You make the things I do company policy?"

God sat pondering this for a moment before replying, "Well, I suppose you'll just have to try harder."

They both sat in silence. Lucifer eventually added, "But..."

"Yes?" God responded immediately with a smile.

"That's not fair."

God's smile slowly melted into a frown. He sighed, "Lucifer." God paused, staring at Lucifer before finishing the thought, "Sometimes ... life isn't fair."

They sat there, saying nothing for several minutes, observing each other. Not ending the silence, Lucifer eventually got out of his chair and slowly made his way out of the office. Passing by God's secretary, he stopped and turned to her. He considered talking to her, but he quickly dropped that train of thought and just walked past her desk. She made no indication of noticing him. He then continued to the elevator and pressed the button.

After his failed attempt at rebellion, Lucifer spent the remainder of his day in a very somber mood. He performed his duties in a daze, unaware of his surroundings, hardly even saying anything to Raphael. The workday finished, and Lucifer walked home slowly. He attempted to contemplate his next move, but it was to no avail. He came to his apartment building, walked past his mailbox without even having the energy to check it, and meandered his way up the stairs and to his apartment. He opened the door, slowly walked inside, sat down on his couch, and silently stayed right there, alone, his mind completely blank.

It was hunger that drove him out of his stupor. He got up and walked into the kitchen. Opening a cupboard, Lucifer noticed that it was almost empty, only part of a box of soda crackers gracing the barren space. Closing the cupboard, he turned to his refrigerator. Unfortunately, doing so uncovered the same problem; he saw only mustard, the end of a bottle of salad dressing, a carton of milk — which he knew contained only maybe a quarter of a glass — and some lettuce that was long past its prime.

He really didn't want to go grocery shopping right now, but what was he going to do, eat mustard and crackers? He let out a large sigh. It wasn't that the grocery store was very far away, either; he just lacked the energy to go there. He slowly shuffled his way toward his entryway; it took immense strength and concentration to take each step. He eventually grabbed his jacket and regained his composure sufficiently to be seen by other angels without ruining his inexistent social status. Ready as he'd ever be, he went back outside.

Because the grocery store was only a block away, he arrived there very quickly. Lucifer briskly rushed through the aisles and made it his intention to grab what he needed swiftly and head back home as fast as he could. He didn't even take the time to compare prices among brands as he usually would.

He approached the only open checkout and started laying his items on the counter, waiting for the cashier to finish ringing in the angel ahead of him. Lucifer tried not to eavesdrop, but he couldn't help it; the cashier was extremely chipper, to the extent that it was hard to ignore.

"...and two more cents makes twenty," the cashier said to the other angel, adding, "And, sir, could you please do me a favor ... and have yourself a great day?"

Ugh, Lucifer thought. He most certainly was not in the mood for this right now.

Approaching the till with caution, Lucifer watched the angel start scanning his items. The cashier immediately looked upon Lucifer with a huge smile. "Why, hello there," he said.

Lucifer merely nodded. The cashier looked over the items he was scanning, saying, "Ooh, two different types of cheese? *Someone* has an appreciation for the finer things. None of that for me, though. Mozzarella is enough excitement for this angel."

Despite the great extent that he went to remain miserable, Lucifer couldn't help but smile. He looked at the angel's nametag and said, "Isaac?"

"Oh, please, call me Zack," the angel responded immediately, still wearing his large grin.

"Zack ... I couldn't help but notice how cheerful an individual you appear to be," Lucifer continued. "You must be having a very good day."

"Well, to tell you the truth," Isaac leaned in closer to finish his thought, "today's been a bit of a challenge."

Lucifer chuckled, "So you say."

Isaac backed up a bit, nonchalantly adding, "No, I'm serious." With that, he went back to scanning items.

Lucifer looked behind himself, confirming he wasn't holding anyone up, then continued the conversation. "But you're so ... happy. I'm kind of surprised that you'd be this cheerful if today's been a bit of a challenge."

Isaac shrugged, "I guess I'm just a happy kind of guy."

Lucifer said nothing.

"To be fair, it's not just that," Isaac continued. "I'm of the philosophy that I'm the basis of how good or bad my day is. If I get up on the wrong side of the bed and I'm grouchy all day, of course things aren't going to go well. So, I figure that adopting a positive attitude is going to help right there. But some days, that isn't even enough. No matter how hard you try, things just don't work — you spend all day trying to force a square into a circle, and you're right where you were when the day began. You get really frustrated, and you try and try and try but nothing seems to help."

“In that case, what do you do?” asked Lucifer.

Isaac shrugged again, “Try harder.”

Lucifer didn’t know what to say.

After paying, Lucifer rushed home and made it his goal not to let today defeat him. Cooking, eating, and cleaning gave him plenty of time to consider his next act of rebellion. By the end of the evening, he came up with a plan: He would not show up for work tomorrow. *God may change company policy to stop my less-than-stellar attempts at rebelling,* he thought, *but what can He do about this? Make a Don’t Come In to Work Day? Good luck; I’d like to see Him try and ruin this one.*

Lucifer woke up when he normally would to go to work, and he performed his usual daily routines. Instead of leaving for work, however, he sat down on his couch and cracked open a new novel that he had been meaning to start for some time. He looked at the large clock on his wall and thought, *Well, I’m sure I’ll be getting a phone call any time now.*

He continued reading, and then casually glanced up at the clock again. Half an hour had passed since he last looked. *How odd,* he thought, *I really would have expected someone to call by now. Oh well.*

He read for another fifteen minutes. There was still no phone call. Lucifer grew far more concerned by this point. He stopped reading and found himself pacing the room. Quite some time passed, and he grew much more edgy; every sound the clock made seemed to taunt him as the hands moved at a snail’s pace. *Maybe I’ll give Raphael a call and see what’s going on,* he thought.

He called Raphael’s phone at the office. It rang several times, but no one answered. Lucifer hung up the phone. *Well, maybe he’s in a meeting or something, he thought. I’m sure I’ll hear from him eventually.*

Lucifer tried to go back to his book, but he found it extremely hard to concentrate. He went back to pacing the room again for some time, then took to reorganizing his newly stocked cupboards, removing everything, putting it all back in, and repeating this process several times until the space was properly optimized.

After a few long hours, Lucifer decided to carefully clean his coffee table, thoroughly scrubbing every inch of it. The phone finally rang, startling him. He picked it up as quickly as he could, dropping it with a loud bang in the process. Picking it back up, he found Raphael's voice at the other end.

"Hey there, Lucifer, how's it going?" Raphael said.

"Raphael? Are you returning my call?" Lucifer asked with a frantic tone in his voice.

There was a pause. Raphael eventually said, "No ... I just phoned to see if you wanted to go for a bike ride. I figured, if you haven't eaten yet—"

"Bike ride?" Lucifer cut him off, "Aren't you supposed to be at work?"

Another pause followed that comment. Raphael replied, "What are you talking about? Didn't you get the memo?"

"Memo? What memo?"

Raphael continued, "I don't know, it was in my mailbox when I got home, so I assumed everyone got one." There was another pause. "Wait, but you *are* at home, and you didn't get the memo? What's going on, Lucifer?"

"I'm rebelling," Lucifer answered quickly. "What did the memo say?"

It took a moment for Raphael to continue speaking. He eventually said, "Um, they sent out random surveys and did some audits on performance and satisfaction. Everything's going as planned — a bit ahead of schedule, you'll be glad to know — so God said we can have a second day of rest."

LUCIFER

Lucifer's heart stopped.

Raphael continued, "Isn't that exciting? A two-day weekend! So, are you coming biking or not?"

Chapter 5

Time for a Change

Raphael sat at a lonely table in the Pearly Gates, swirling his drink around slowly. He appeared to be staring attentively at the spinning ice within the liquid, while, in actuality, his mind was completely bereft of thought as he gazed at the various shapes dancing before him. His eyes grew unfocused. The jumble before him continued to live a life of its own, but it was nothing more than an incomprehensible blur before him.

Eventually, he stopped the motion of his hand, the contents of the glass taking some time to catch up to the command, still circling.

Raphael sighed and brought the glass up to his lips, taking a sip.

"What's wrong with you?"

Raphael looked up to find Peter standing next to him.

Peter continued, "I never see you here alone. You got a temperature?"

Peter stopped talking to give Raphael some time to respond. Raphael smiled, slowly putting his glass down before conversing. Eventually, he quietly said, “I’m just waiting.”

He looked away from Peter, continuing, “Max, another angel from my department, wanted to meet with me. Apparently, it’s really important, so I came here pretty fast.”

Returning his gaze to Peter, he went on, “Not that I have to go very far to get here, but you know. He’s keeping me waiting and, to be perfectly honest, I’m getting bored.”

“Well, if it’s important,” Peter said, “it’s probably worth waiting for.”

“I hope you’re right.” Raphael looked at his watch, “I mean, I’ve been sitting here twenty minutes already.”

Peter smiled at him, adding, “Stick it out; you won’t regret it.”

Raphael laughed, “I’ll tell you what, I’ll stick around until I finish my drink. If he’s not here by then, he can meet with me another time.”

“I’ll tell *you* what,” Peter said with a sly grin on his face, pointing at Raphael as he did so. Intrigued, Raphael leaned in a bit closer to hear what Peter had to say. Peter continued, “Let’s make a bet. If your friend’s not here by the time you finish that drink...”

Raphael picked it up and looked at it.

Peter finished his sentence, “...it’s on the house.”

“However,” Peter leaned back a bit and put his finger up as he said this, “if there’s even a drop left in there by the time ... Max ... shows up, you have to buy a drink for him. Deal?”

Raphael swished his drink around a bit more, “I don’t know, Pete, I’m already halfway done. This doesn’t seem like a good bet on your part, but I’m game.”

Peter nodded and began walking away. As he moved, he turned to Raphael and added, “And no chugging it; I want to see you drinking it at a reasonable pace.”

Raphael laughed, "Don't worry. I want this to be a sporting bet." He considered what he was saying before adding, with another chuckle, "You're not going to make me eat the ice, right?"

Peter barely made it across the floor and down to the bar when a slender blonde angel walked in, looking around. Raphael glanced over and saw that it was, in fact, Maxwell. Maxwell appeared lost for only a moment; seeing Raphael, he gave him a large smile and a wave. Raphael waved back, and Maxwell started walking over.

"Crap," Raphael muttered under his breath.

Approaching the table, Maxwell said, "Hey, Raphael. I'm glad you could make it. I hope I didn't keep you waiting too long."

"No, not at all," replied Raphael. "Here, sit down. I'll buy you a drink."

"No, no. That's okay," Maxwell responded immediately, taking the seat as he did so.

"Please, Max ... I insist." Upon speaking, Raphael smiled up at Peter, who was now behind Maxwell, ready and waiting for his drink request. Raphael continued, "I don't like to drink alone."

Maxwell shrugged and said, "Fair enough. I'll have a gin and tonic."

Peter nodded, saying, "You got it. I'll whip it up in a jiffy."

With Peter now walking back to the bar, Raphael asked, "So, Max, what's this big important project you wanted me to help you with?"

"I guess the best way for me to put it is..." Maxwell trailed off as he considered the proper words. "Landscape management."

"What do you mean?"

Maxwell leaned in a bit closer and licked his lips before elaborating, "You know how God said He wanted the whole world to be a living and changing being in its own right?"

Raphael nodded.

Seeing this, Maxwell continued what he was saying, "And none of us down at the R&D landscape division really knew a good way to—"

Peter came back at this time and placed the drink on the table next to Maxwell, who nodded. Peter then left them alone once again.

Maxwell continued his train of thought, "We couldn't think up a good way to approach it. All the angels in the department figured we'd have to just keep going back and changing things around and touching things up as time goes on."

"Well, yes," Raphael interjected, "I can't think of a better way to ... alter the landscapes that I designed."

Maxwell smiled, adding, "I have. Landscape management."

Raphael shook his head. "But that doesn't mean anything to me."

Maxwell looked both ways and leaned close to Raphael again before continuing. "To be honest, I'm just conceptualizing the idea right now; it's just in its infancy. But the basic plan is to take the different forces and elements that we set up throughout the world and use them to shape the landscapes. You know, have the wind and water slowly wear away at the hills and mountains."

Raphael opened his mouth, but Maxwell went on, "Of course, when I say 'slow,' I mean really, really slow. The casual observer won't notice it in action on a day-to-day basis, but it will be happening. No, it's more like — if you took a picture of the landscape and then looked at the same thing fifty, a hundred, a thousand years later, *that's* when you'd notice a big difference."

Maxwell stopped to ensure Raphael was more or less following him. Raphael nodded, at which point Maxwell said, "With the program, we'd be living up to God's standards; we would have the world we place the humans in molding itself all around them, all on its own. As a plus, we'd also be making things a lot easier for ourselves. Think about it: You can just set up the landscapes, turn on the program, and let it go. Then we can just sit back and watch it do its thing."

Raphael considered it and sighed. "I think you might be on to something. Have you thought about how much time this program is going to take to get up and running? I mean, I still have quite a few landscapes to design."

Maxwell frowned, "I have thought about it, but I really can't say. I'm hoping that it works out well from the get-go, but it may take a lot of work to tweak it to our liking. Keep in mind, more work now means less work later on ... virtually no work later on, in fact."

Raphael nodded again, asking, "What are you calling this program?"

Maxwell shrugged, "I was kind of thinking of calling it Erosion."

"Erosion?" Raphael's eyebrows went up, "What's that supposed to mean?"

"Well, I figured that 'eroding' kind of sounded like the elements slowly wearing away at the landscape," Maxwell answered. "It has a kind of ring to it."

"Fair enough," Raphael replied. "Anyway, I'm going to take off. Why don't we meet sometime at the start of next week? We can get down some ideas and get started on things. Of course, we'll have to book the geo-cultivation room and see how things hold up."

"Of course," replied Maxwell.

They both finished their drinks and stood up.

"Until then," Raphael added.

Ding! The elevator doors opened, and out stepped Lucifer. His mind was absolutely blank. Out of instinct, he walked directly to his office, where Raphael was already hard at work.

"Oh ... my ... goodness," Raphael said slowly and expressively.

Lucifer looked shocked and asked, "What?"

He received no answer. Growing annoyed quickly, he tried again. "*What?*"

Raphael just sat in silence for a moment, looking Lucifer up and down. He then ended the stillness, pointing his pen at Lucifer, "Now ... I wouldn't have been able to tell by looking at you..."

Lucifer just stood at the doorway, confusion plastered all over his face.

"But you made one large mistake." Raphael paused, leaving Lucifer dumbfounded. "Tell me what you did with him," he continued.

Lucifer hesitated. A hint of annoyance still graced his voice. "What I did with *whom?*"

Raphael raised his eyebrows, as though it should be obvious, saying, "Lucifer."

"What in the heavens are you talking about?"

Raphael lowered his eyebrows and frowned, explaining, "Like I said, you pulled off his appearance very well." He continued, pointing his pen directly at Lucifer after each point he made, "But, Lucifer has never, *ever,* not *once* been late to work since I've been working with him."

Silence once again. Raphael smiled from ear to ear. As Lucifer slowly began to understand what was happening, a grin gradually grew on his face as well.

"I had you going for a minute there," Raphael said as Lucifer took his seat.

Lucifer opened his briefcase. He sat quietly for a second and then told Raphael, "You're just lucky my mind's been on this rebelling business, otherwise I wouldn't have fallen for it." He stopped and thought about his comment, adding, "In fact, what am I saying? If it wasn't for this rebelling business, I would have been sitting in this office before you even got here!"

Raphael just kept grinning. "So, Rebel, what's on the agenda for today?" he said as he crumpled up a piece of paper and threw it at the garbage can.

Lucifer shrugged, "Oh, I don't—"

"Swish!" Raphael interrupted, as the paper landed squarely in the can.

Lucifer waited to ensure Raphael was done with what he was saying. Seeing Raphael waiting patiently for him to continue, he did so. "I don't know, nothing too exciting. I think I'm just going to try to iron out a few problems that have surfaced with some of the human models we've been working with. They're winding up so ... unnatural. It's not going to be easy since everyone seems to be on board with making polite robots. I probably won't see any real results until next week."

He considered it momentarily and then finished his thought, "Maybe the week after."

"Don't tell me you forgot about your meeting with Marketing in, oh..." Raphael paused, looking at his watch. "Forty-five minutes."

Lucifer was puzzled once again. He looked at Raphael, then to the clock up on the wall. His glance quickly turned to the words *Meeting with Marketing,* highlighted and underlined several times, next to ten o'clock in his agenda on his desk, at which point he replied, "Of course not."

Lucifer felt his eyes slowly closing. Realizing he was drifting off to sleep, he jumped a bit and awakened himself with a jolt. He looked around, but it appeared as though no one had noticed; everyone was enthralled by Nathaniel's presentation. The more he considered it, the more he wasn't too surprised by that fact. The presentation was very flashy; Marketing angels really had a flair for making slideshows that exhibited information in a way that was pleasing to the eye, and for getting angels excited no matter how drab or inconsequential the information presented actually was.

He really wasn't sure why he was there. None of the presentation had anything to do with him.

"So as you can see," Nathaniel said, "this is where it's all going to start. We're going to put those first two humans, Adam and Eve, in what I have named the 'Garden of Eden.' Let me take you there. Just imagine it. The Garden will have warm weather all day long." Using a laser pointer, he started to give them a tour. "See the lovely brook flowing with fresh water, giving life to the numerous, blossoming trees; on the trees, enormous, ripe fruit for our humans to enjoy."

He stopped for a moment and let them take it all in.

"Now, for some reason," he paused again before making this point, "Michael tells me that the ... Big Man upstairs ... doesn't want the humans eating from one particular apple tree."

The angels looked surprised and started muttering amongst themselves. One asked, "So, why even put it in the Garden?"

Nathaniel laughed, "I know, I asked Michael the same thing, but apparently God just wants it in there so, of course, that's the way it's got to be."

The other angels laughed along with him. Nathaniel waited for things to simmer down before continuing, "So, that's where we came in. We had a design meeting with R&D and came up with this scheme, the 'forbidden tree' being over here."

He circled it with his pointer. “Why here, you ask? We got them to program the humans’ taste in such a way to prefer certain foods over others. We placed a cluster of the more desirables around this area, which is where we’re going to place the humans. As you move out of the area, the food becomes less and less enjoyable to them, with the apple tree in this back area, here. We performed some test simulations and saw that the humans stuck to the desirable area overall. There was slight venturing out, but they kept coming back when they got out here; they didn’t even come close to the apple tree. I double-checked with Manufacturing, and they liked the layout.”

“But, what if they still eat it?” another angel asked. “I mean, even if they don’t like the taste of apples, there’s still a chance that they’ll try them once. How are we going to make sure they know it’s not allowed?”

Nathaniel smiled, “Don’t worry about that. Marketing will get the message across one way or another. Plus, R&D will have to add it to their programming; it’s a start to fix their taste buds, but we need to ensure they do as they’re told. If we give them actual choices, it might not work out, but my buddy Lucy’s going to take care of that, right?”

The daydreaming Lucifer jolted to life once more as Nathaniel singled him out. He gave an awkward smile, but said nothing, and Nathaniel went back to his presentation. Lucifer really wasn’t happy about this; it meant other departments were on the same page about human personality.

As Nathaniel kept talking, Lucifer continued watching him, but he wasn’t listening to the words that were coming out of his mouth. It was bothering him – Nathaniel’s mouth moved in slow motion. Every incomprehensible sound that came out jabbed him right in the chest. It was as though his presentation morphed into a new one, all in Lucifer’s mind. Another smile slowly formed on Nathaniel’s face. He looked right at Lucifer, and Lucifer swore he could hear him say, in a very low tone, "I will ruin the project."

At that very moment, Lucifer knew what he had to do. Nathaniel was in mid-sentence when Lucifer suddenly interrupted with a simple, quiet, "No."

The presentation stopped immediately. The room fell silent. With confusion all over his face, Nathaniel asked, "Excuse me?"

Lucifer took a moment to look around at all the staring angels. He considered what he was saying, and then, in a slightly louder voice, he said, "No."

The silence continued among the rest of the angels in the room, so quiet they only now could hear the whirring of the projector. Nathaniel said, "I don't follow you."

Lucifer clarified his position, shakily, "No ... I'm not ... going to take care of that."

The other angels began to look at each other, bewildered. Nathaniel glanced at a nearby angel. Grinning, he rolled his eyes, and turned his gaze back to Lucifer, telling him, "Lucy, baby, I don't think you understand—"

"No, Nathaniel," Lucifer cut him off.

The angels looked back at Lucifer; the smile dropped off Nathaniel's face.

Lucifer continued, in a much harsher tone, "I don't think *you* understand."

Standing at the front of the quiet room, Nathaniel cleared his throat. He added, "No ... I guess I don't ... understand."

Lucifer looked around him at all the other silent angels. He went on, "Nathaniel, you're missing the point. You're *all* missing the point. This project wasn't intended to ... to ... test our robot-making skills." He stopped for a second, but no one else dared to say anything. "God doesn't want us to just make mindless automations," he said. "We might as well just make Him some toys to play with, if that's what we're intending on doing."

Lucifer opened his briefcase and began putting his papers away. Looking down, he added, "I don't think you could have missed the point harder if you were blindfolded and dizzy."

He grabbed his things and stood up. Looking around the room again, Lucifer said, with a small wave, "I would say that I would love to stay and chat with you about this subject all day, but that would be a lie, and I have another important engagement to attend to."

With that, he opened the door and left the conference room. He began walking down the hall, but Nathaniel came rushing after him. When he caught up, Nathaniel grabbed Lucifer's arm. Lucifer quickly spun around, now facing Nathaniel and the open door of the conference room. Stepping in close, Nathaniel whispered, "What are you doing to me?"

Lucifer jerked his arm free.

Nathaniel continued whispering, "Lucy, baby, don't be like this."

Lucifer was visibly unimpressed; he said, "By the way, my name's Lucifer."

Nathaniel failed to hide his frustration, saying, "Yes, okay, fine." But catching himself, he quickly pulled himself together. Nathaniel realized how much he needed to get Lucifer to understand the importance of his idea. In a much gentler tone, he added, "Lucifer, I told Michael this was all figured out. You *need* to help me..." He looked behind himself, into the conference room, and then back at Lucifer, finishing the thought with pleading eyes. "...Or he's going to chew me out for sure."

"Nathaniel." Lucifer paused, looking him up and down, his voice drenched in annoyance as he eventually spoke, "Please don't tell me how to do my job. I'm doing what's best for the project."

"You don't know that," interjected Nathaniel quickly.

"Well, neither do you, and to be perfectly frank, you aren't qualified to make decisions pertaining to my work," Lucifer retorted.

They stood in silence, then Nathaniel quietly added, “But that’s not fair.”

“Sometimes life isn’t fair.”

With that, Lucifer turned around and walked away. He managed to maintain his composure, but he felt chills run up his spine. There was something about having God’s words echoing out of his own mouth that didn’t sit well with him.

Chatter was coming from the conference room as angels wondered aloud what they had just witnessed. One looked out the door, seeing Nathaniel’s back as he stood in the hallway watching Lucifer walk away.

Lucifer walked down the hallway, eyes forward. Other angels passed him as he went, but he didn’t even acknowledge their presence. Making it to the elevator, he pressed the Down button and waited patiently, his mind completely blank.

Ding! The elevator doors opened, and he stepped inside the empty box. He moved his finger over the button for the fourteenth floor. He almost pressed it, but just left it hovering there for a moment. The doors closed as he continued to hesitate. He just sat there glancing over the tall panel of buttons and down to the number fourteen, partially covered by his finger, not really knowing why he was finding it so hard to just press it and go back to his office. He scanned the panel once more, all the way up to the number ninety-six, alone at the top. His finger still remaining where it was, he fixed his gaze at the top button. Slowly, he moved his finger, up and up, higher and higher, until it was now hovering over number ninety-six. He hesitated only a moment before pressing it in. The button lit up, and the elevator once more came to life.

Lucifer could feel the elevator moving, pulling him higher and higher. As he went, he could feel his chest tightening. The closer to the top it brought him, the tighter his chest became. He still could not fathom what possessed him to go to the top floor; he definitely had no desire to see God right now, but something beckoned him. Nearing the floor, his uneasiness grew so much that he was finding it hard to breathe. He started to feel dizzy and began to lose his footing.

Ding! The elevator doors slid open, and Lucifer stood completely motionless, not saying a word. From inside the elevator, aside from the far, plain wall, all he could make out was the edge of God's secretary's desk. He took a single step forward, his anxiety somewhat lessening. The doors began to close, but he reached his hand out in time to trigger the sensor. They opened once more, and out stepped Lucifer, very unsure of himself.

He slowly walked up to the secretary's desk, peering across to God's door, which was open.

The secretary looked up from her crossword puzzle, giving Lucifer a pleasant smile, showing off the pearly whites of her perfect teeth. "Hello there," she said.

Lucifer nearly died when she spoke. Her voice was more pleasing to his ears than he had ever imagined, light and delicate. *Be still, my heart,* Lucifer thought. He wanted to say something eloquent, to leave a good first impression, but all he managed to squeak out was a small, "Hi."

The smile left her face. "Was God expecting to see you?" she inquired. Looking down at an agenda on her desk, she continued, "I don't see any meetings on His schedule at this time. If you want, I can see if He's busy right now."

She started to get up out of her chair, when Lucifer stopped her, "Oh, no, that's alright, actually. I didn't really come up here to see God."

A small smile crept back onto her face, but Lucifer could see that she was confused. “Oh?” She paused for a moment before adding, “Then why are you up here?”

I don’t really know, he thought. His mouth caught up to his thoughts, and he blurted out, “I don’t really know.”

The smile was once again leaving her face, and she opened her mouth to speak, when he continued, “I don’t really know how to say this—” He stopped, looking down to read her name plate. “—Mary, but I actually came up here to ... ask you something.”

She hesitated. He could see that nothing like this had ever happened to her before, but he wasn’t entirely surprised, strange as it was for him as well. She eventually said, “Okay?”

He looked back down at her desk, slightly swaying his briefcase back and forth as he spoke, “You see, I’ve been coming up here from time to time, and I couldn’t really help ... noticing you on the way by. Not to say that we said anything to each other until now, but that’s okay.”

He knew that he was starting to ramble, so he tried extremely hard to focus his thoughts, “What I mean to say is ... it’s okay if you don’t want to, but I was wondering if you would ... maybe, like to...” Lucifer looked her back in the eyes. Mary was listening attentively, waiting for him to come out with it. He took a deep breath and continued, “...go out some time?”

She smiled again. “You mean like on a date?” she asked him.

“Well, no...” he added. “Yes ... no...”

She looked confused once again.

He went on, “What I mean to say is, it doesn’t *have* to be a *date,* exactly.”

She frowned. “So, what are you asking me, then?”

He looked at the floor. “I’m sorry. I’m just not very good at this. Just ... never mind.” Lucifer turned suddenly and started walking away, adding, “Just forget I said anything.”

"No, Lucifer," Mary reached out to Lucifer, her fingers extended toward him, and he stopped walking. "If you are trying to ask me out on a date, I would love to."

Lucifer couldn't believe what she said. A huge smile came to his face. He wanted to tell her how happy he was, but he was speechless. She motioned for him to come closer to the desk, and he happily obliged. She clicked her pen and wrote on a small piece of paper, saying, "Here, it's my number. Take it."

Once again, he did exactly what Mary said. He put his briefcase up on the desk and opened it with a click. Folding the paper carefully, he placed it inside the briefcase, closing it afterwards, and continued his gigantic smile. Lucifer nodded once to her and made his way back to the elevator, pressing the button. As the doors opened, he waved and said, "I'll call you."

He stepped inside and pressed the button for the fourteenth floor. As the doors began to close, he called out, "I'll *definitely* call you."

She snickered to herself, replying with a small wave, "Okay, Lucifer."

Blueprints lay spread across Raphael's desk, overlapping each other in a way that they appeared, to the untrained eye, to be an unorganized mess. It was just the way Raphael worked; when he started that morning, he began the design of a specific mountain peak, meticulously mapping out every crevasse, only to get inspiration for half a mile of coastline. Pulling out a fresh blueprint and drawing for around half an hour would cause him to realize that a valley would be the perfect addition to a previous mountain range, so he would rummage around his files to bring out that blueprint in order to improve it. As such, he eventually wound up with a jumbled mess of blueprints strewn about his work area, jumping from one to the other, tweaking and tinkering.

When Raphael got going in such a fashion, it generally took much effort to rouse him back into the real world. However, this particular day was an exception. Lucifer threw his briefcase down onto his desk with a loud bang, causing Raphael to jump about a foot in the air.

“Jesus!” shouted Raphael.

Lucifer looked at him with a perplexed smile on his face. With a bit of a laugh, he asked, “What did you just say?”

The confusion spread to Raphael as well. He pondered it momentarily before responding, “I don’t know.”

Lucifer laughed again, “Is that even a real word?”

“I couldn’t really say.”

They both looked to the floor and shared a bit of a chuckle. Suddenly, Lucifer came back to his senses and said, “Oh! So, you’ll never guess where *I’ve* been.”

Raphael thought about it briefly and then responded, “Meeting with Marketing?”

The smile left Lucifer’s face and his voice lost its excited tone. “Well, yes.” Raphael’s question stopped him dead in his tracks, but only briefly. He then remembered what he had to say, bringing back his excitement. He continued, “But *after* the meeting, *this* angel totally went up to the ninety-sixth floor.”

“To see—”

“Not to see God,” Lucifer quickly interrupted, bringing his hand forward with his index finger up.

He paused again for effect, not moving his hand. Raphael patiently waited to hear the end of the anecdote. Feeling the growing level of anticipation, Lucifer went on. “No, I went upstairs, and I asked God’s secretary out.”

Raphael’s eyes widened as this bombshell was revealed.

Lucifer finished his thought with a shout, “And she fucking – whoop!” He put his hand to his own mouth. He then moved his hand slightly, as though he needed to allow the quiet words of his whisper to escape. "She fucking said yes."

Raphael quickly got up out of his chair and patted Lucifer firmly on the arm twice. "Good job, buddy. See? What did I tell you?" Still not really believing what he had just heard, Raphael shook his head. "What in Heaven possessed you to ask her out?" he asked.

"I don't really know," said Lucifer, swelling with pride due to the nature of his accomplishment. "I guess I was kind of ... fired up after that meeting."

Raphael put his hands on his hips. He glanced down at the floor, shaking his head once again. Looking back up at Lucifer, Raphael added, "So, what are you going to do on your date?"

Lucifer looked past Raphael. Fixing his gaze on the far wall, his smile slowly melted off his face.

Raphael grew concerned. "What?"

He received no response.

"Was it something I said?" Raphael asked, turning to look at the wall behind him. Not seeing anything out of the ordinary, he returned his gaze to Lucifer.

Lucifer continued looking at the wall, which now grew out of focus. A look of horror covered his face, and he quietly muttered, "She said yes."

Raphael, still confused, smiled an uneasy smile, adding, "Yeah?"

Lucifer looked back at Raphael, still wearing the look of complete dread. In a panic, he repeated, "She said yes." After a slight pause, he asked, "What have I done?"

Turning, he started pacing back and forth, his rate of breathing steadily increasing. Raphael grew worried, not exactly sure what to say to Lucifer.

"This is bad. This is very, very bad," Lucifer said quickly without stopping for a breath, still pacing to and fro. "I haven't been on a date in forever. I don't know what to say or do. I'm totally going to blow it ... This is very bad."

Raphael put his palms out toward Lucifer. In as reassuring a tone as he could muster, Raphael said, "Calm down. You'll be fine. You just have to be yourself."

"Myself?" Lucifer responded immediately, stopping his pacing and looking back at Raphael. "How can you say that? I can't just be myself! Myself is awkward. Myself is nervous and boring ... *Myself* will blow it."

"Relax," Raphael continued.

"Relax? How can I relax?" Lucifer shouted.

Raphael ignored the comment and finished his thought. "She must like the real you. You weren't acting unnatural when you talked to her, right?"

Lucifer thought about it briefly, "I guess not ... maybe a bit ... I was pretty nervous at the time."

"See what I mean? When the time comes, just have a few drinks to calm yourself down, and you'll be fine."

"But what will I talk about?"

"It doesn't matter," Raphael responded as quickly as he could. "Just talk about things that interest you, and try to linger on topics that seem to interest her."

"Where will I take her?"

"There's a great new restaurant I found that you can bring her to. Hardly anyone knows about it yet, and it's got amazing food."

"But I have nothing to wear."

Raphael grabbed Lucifer by both shoulders and looked him squarely in the eyes. "Lucifer, I'll take you shopping. Trust me, you'll look fabulous." Raphael stared at Lucifer for a moment, still holding onto his shoulders. He added, "Now will you please calm down?"

Lucifer looked down to the floor, then back at Raphael. He closed his eyes for a few seconds, then reopened them. Still with a concerned look on his face, he nodded slowly. Raphael released his grip, patting him on the shoulder as he did so.

"You'll be fine," Raphael added, with a smile.

Lucifer returned the look with a smile of his own, albeit a nervous one. With that, he slowly made his way to his desk and sat down, Raphael still remaining where he was, smiling. Lucifer opened his briefcase, pulled out some papers, and started working. Content that order was restored, Raphael sat back down at his desk and continued his drawings.

Chapter 6

A Managerial Lunch

Gabriel sat alone in a small cafe a block and a half away from the office building. He liked spending his lunch break there, usually watching the angels constantly walking past the large windows in the front. How he loved to just sit, relax, and watch the heavens pass him by, enjoying the food the cafe provided.

The food! What food it truly was. The angels in the cafe made sandwiches the likes of which the human mind can hardly comprehend. Sure, they were made from familiar ingredients, such as melted brie and apricot jelly, but there was a certain indescribable splendor about them. One bite of a sandwich would drive the senses wild; one spoonful of soup would send an individual to a place better than Heaven. Despite these accolades, however, hardly any patrons tended to grace the diner with their presence. The unfortunate truth was that, in the area of Heaven near the office, speed was embraced much more than quality, particularly where food was concerned. Given that most angels had merely half an hour to eat lunch, they could not stand to wait for their food, no matter the quality, lest they find themselves having only five minutes in which to finish it and hurry back to their floor. As well, the post-lunch congestion would slow down the pace of the elevator to that of a snail; if a hapless angel worked even ten floors up, there was no telling how long the ride would be.

Despite all this, Gabriel had no worries with regards to rushing through lunch. Really, if he was to show up five, ten, fifteen minutes, or even half an hour late, who would question it? He answered to God only, and He never batted an eyelash. Of course, had He made even a small indication of displeasure, Gabriel would never show up even one second late ever again. Luckily for him, as well as the owners of the diner, this wasn't the case.

Rather than watch out the window this lunch, Gabriel sat, oblivious to the world around him, reading a novel while contently slurping his soup. As it happens, Michael, the manager of Marketing, was hurrying past the place at the same time. Peering in the window, Michael saw a hulking angel sitting in the cafe. As such, he stopped to verify it was Gabriel's bulk; looking through the glass, Michael could see that he was not mistaken. He hurried inside, the bell above the door dinging as he did so. Grabbing a chair, he pulled it up to Gabriel's table and sat down.

Gabriel finished the paragraph he was reading before checking to see who had invited himself to join him. Putting the book down, he looked up, "Oh, Michael. How's it going?"

"You know," Michael quickly answered, "busy as always. How about you?"

Gabriel thought about it before responding, "I'm doing fine. Things are running smoothly in R&D."

"Well, that's actually something I wanted to—"

Michael stopped mid-sentence, seeing the waiter standing there patiently waiting to take his order, pen and pad at the ready. “Bring me a coffee,” he said, adding, “and make sure you bring me cream and sugar.”

The waiter jotted it down quickly and left to fetch it. Michael continued, “It’s amazing that I have to ask for cream and sugar when I order a coffee these days, that they don’t automatically bring it. Too often I make an assumption like that and the genius thinks I just want it black. If I say, ‘black,’ then I want it black. Otherwise, bring me the stupid cream.”

Gabriel smiled. Michael looked him up and down. “To tell you the truth, Gabriel, I’m surprised you’re sitting here at this time so happily. Saying that everything’s running smoothly in your department leads me to think that you may be ... oblivious ... to certain matters.”

“What are you trying to say?”

“What do you *think* I’m trying to say?”

Gabriel slowly sipped a spoonful of soup. Upon swallowing, he said, “It sounds like you think I’m not doing my job.”

It was uncommon for Gabriel to take such a tone with him, but Michael was sure it would change if he was assertive enough. He knew that Gabriel was always trying to avoid conflict. Michael continued, “Well, sometimes it appears as though R&D is chugging along like a...” Michael paused, considering the best way to finish his thought. “Ship without a captain.”

Gabriel lowered his eyebrows, “Things run better in R&D when I’m not breathing down everyone’s neck. I can trust my angels to do a good job in the end.”

Michael shrugged, nonchalantly adding, “So you say.”

The waiter came back with Michael’s coffee. Placing it on the table in front of him, he left them alone once more. Gabriel watched the waiter come and go, then looked back at Michael, trying to figure out where he was going with this conversation. They sat in silence, Gabriel eating his soup as he stared at Michael. Michael opened up a package of cream, dumping it in and stirring. He blew on his coffee, taking a sip, saying, "Ooh, that's hot."

"What in Heaven are you talking about?" Gabriel finally asked.

Michael looked down at his coffee and back at Gabriel, "My coffee is hot. Not that I'm complaining; I like it that way."

"No, no, forget about the coffee. I'm talking about what you were just mentioning ... this 'ship without a captain' stuff," clarified Gabriel.

"Well, I'm glad you asked," continued Michael, putting his coffee back down on the table. "You see, there's been an incident."

"An incident?"

"Yes." Michael paused, and then quietly repeated, "An incident."

Gabriel gave a small shrug. He opened his mouth to speak, but Michael cut him off, "You see, a formal complaint was filed by one of my guys against one of your guys."

"On the basis of what?"

"It seems that your guy was impeding the work of my guy." Michael paused once more. He went on, "And I don't think I need to tell you how busy I am. I don't have time for this crap."

Gabriel started to speak, but Michael cut him off once more, loudly adding, "None of us have time for this crap, Gabriel. This incident really set us back."

"Okay, okay," Gabriel's tone was much gentler as he tried his best to diffuse the situation. "How bad is this incident? What happened?"

"What happened? My guy had a great idea — I should know; I cleared it — and he got your guy on board to make it happen. Apparently, your guy said he'd help him out and get everything moving, but he changes his mind and goes back on the promise he made to my guy."

Gabriel didn't know what to say. "Wow ... I—"

“Not *only* that,” Michael cut him off again, “but *your* guy drops this bombshell in the middle of *my* guy’s presentation. And it wasn’t a simple, ‘Sorry, I don’t think I can do that anymore,’ or anything; he humiliated him in front of all the other angels.”

“I’m ... speechless. I apologize for everything.”

Michael leaned in closer, quietly adding, “Gabriel, an apology won’t fix this. I need you to tell me that you’ll sort this all out.”

“Of course. I’ll definitely get to the bottom of this. Who was the complaint filed against?”

Michael looked down at his coffee, then back into Gabriel’s eyes, saying, “His name is Lucifer. You know him?”

Gabriel leaned back a bit and considered what Michael just said. “Lucifer?” Gabriel didn’t really believe his ears. He asked, “Are you sure?”

“Do I *look* like I’m sure?” Michael asked.

Gabriel said nothing.

Seeing that he needed to go through the unfortunate trouble of explaining his rhetorical question, Michael quickly added, “Yes, I’m sure — of course I’m sure!”

Gabriel silently reflected for another moment before saying, “Because ... Lucifer’s good. He really puts out great work, and he’s pretty ... non-confrontational. You must be mistaken.”

“I assure you that I’m not.”

Gabriel looked at his soup and shook his head. “If you say so ... I guess I’ll have a talk with him.”

“See that you do. We have a well-oiled machine here; we don’t need any worn-out parts.” With that, Michael pulled a few coins from his pocket and forcibly placed them on the table, leaving the cafe. Gabriel merely sat there, staring at his soup, considering what he should do. He couldn’t allow any R&D angels to create such disturbances, but he really did find it hard to believe that Lucifer would be the cause. He picked up his book again and continued eating his soup.

He tried to read, but he was finding that his mind was elsewhere. The more he considered it, the less he believed that Lucifer was the cause of the problem. He knew deep in his heart that Lucifer was a good angel. Besides, Gabriel didn't really want to cause a disturbance within his own department. The longer he sat, it seemed less and less necessary to give Lucifer a talking-to. By the end of his lunch, Gabriel came to a decision that he would avoid any confrontation at this time. He knew he told Michael that it would be dealt with, but now he was unsure that there was even a problem to begin with. Of course, he would have to act if any other complaint came in, but he was positive that this would be the last he heard of it.

Chapter 7

Date Night

When Raphael reassured Lucifer that he would set him up and make him look fabulous, he wasn't kidding around. By the time Raphael was done with him after a long day of shopping, Lucifer was exhausted and his wallet felt quite a bit lighter, but it was well worth it. At the end of the day, Lucifer was fitted with a lovely new suit; dark as it was, it really came together with the fiery red of his hair to make him stand out. It made him tall, dark, and handsome, in the words of Raphael. But the suit was only the beginning. Raphael got him to buy the whole package: new jacket, new shoes, new pocket watch. The look was completed with cuff links, suspenders, and a dark fedora, which Raphael was particularly proud of. He wanted Lucifer to hide the hair until they arrived at the restaurant. Lucifer would enter the restaurant; as he took off the fedora, the whole look would suddenly pop, making everyone notice Mister Tall, Dark, and Handsome. He had the look; it would then just be up to Lucifer not to hold back if he wanted to win Mary over.

Lucifer picked up Mary, and they walked over to the restaurant. He could feel his nerves taking over as they went; he barely said a word to her the entire way there. At one point, he did manage to say that she was simply stunning, but he received no response from her. He couldn't be sure if she had actually heard him; it was more of a mumble than anything.

Arriving at the restaurant, Lucifer helped Mary with her coat, and his eyes nearly popped out of their sockets. She wore a simple black dress that clung tightly against her. How exquisite she was. She carried herself in a manner delicate as a flower swaying in a gentle breeze, with effortless grace; she was petite, yet her figure firm as the ground upon which they now stood. Just a glance at any part of her body brought forth strong desire in Lucifer. He struggled to suppress the urge to stare; he struggled to suppress the growing tightness in his trousers.

He stood observing her for only a second, but it felt like an eternity to Lucifer. Growing embarrassed at the notion of freezing in place for some time, he felt it would be in his best interest to keep moving and remove his coat. It would be tragic to ruin things this early in the outing just because he came across as overly strange. He took off his coat and hat, handing them off to the coat check. Immediately upon doing so, Raphael's plan successfully came to fruition. Although unbeknownst to Lucifer, Mary took notice of the look coming together in a perfect singularity, the result of which was another staring angel.

Lucifer escorted Mary to the table they were directed to; the whole while, both did the best they could not to look at the other, as much as they each desired another glance. They took their seats and started pondering the menus. It was only as Lucifer glanced over the wine list that he caught wind of the situation. He looked up to see Mary staring at him. He smiled.

"You have very ... striking eyes," Lucifer said, his resolve strengthened.

She blushed, returning the smile and looking back down at her menu. He couldn't believe he actually said that; generally that was the sort of thing he might have thought about but would keep to himself. The waiter came to their table, a slender, well-dressed angel with a tiny moustache. He spoke: "Welcome to our humble restaurant. My name is Samuel, and I will be your waiter for this evening. Have the two of you decided on a wine?"

Lucifer looked back down at the wine list, then up to Mary. He asked, "Do you have a preference?"

"Oh, no. I don't really know a lot about wine. You decide."

He glanced the list over briefly, then looked to Samuel. "What would you recommend?"

"Why, that really depends on what you desire in a wine. We do have a lovely Merlot that is quite full-bodied," Samuel said, pointing to the list as he spoke. "If you would prefer something lighter, we do have a marvelous Shiraz, bottled in the Cherubim Estates."

Lucifer replied, "I think ... something lighter is in order. Bring us a bottle of the Shiraz."

"Exquisite choice," Samuel added as he backed up, turned, and walked away to fetch them their wine.

Lucifer and Mary looked around the restaurant, avoiding eye contact as best as they could. Lucifer wanted to start a conversation, but he knew not what to say. The awkwardness was short-lived, however, as Samuel came back very quickly, placing a wine glass on the table in front of each of them and opening the bottle with a pop. He poured some wine into Lucifer's glass and stood at attention, patiently awaiting the verdict. Lucifer grabbed the glass and brought it up to his nose, deeply sniffing, noting a hint of berry in the scent. Bringing it to his lips, he sipped the wine, swishing it around in his mouth before swallowing. His pupils widened upon tasting. Lucifer gave Samuel a nod, at which point the waiter poured them each a glass.

Samuel then stood back at attention, asking, "Have you both had a chance to glance over the menus?"

Lucifer looked down to his, "I believe I will try ... the salmon."

Samuel turned to Mary, who also was looking at her menu. "Um ... I will have ... the fettuccini with the peppers and leeks."

"But of course," Samuel replied. "And shall I bring out an appetizer for the two of you?"

"Oh, I was wondering," Mary said immediately, "what is this ... carpaccio?"

Samuel smiled, "Ah, the carpaccio. Our chef cuts thin slices of the most tender veal. It is served raw in an oil, with capers and parmesan. But, I must warn you, you must eat the whole thing, capers, parmesan and all, or else it is just not the same."

Mary had a look of mild disgust, "I don't know ... raw meat?"

"No, we just *have* to try it," Lucifer said right away, his eyes lighting up. "I finally got the nerve to try steak tartare a few months ago, and it was to *die* for."

"Really?" she said. "Well, if you say so. Let's get that."

"*Magnifique,*" Samuel said. "You will not regret it." He then backed up a few steps, turned, and left them alone.

As Mary and Lucifer waited for their food, they once again found it hard to make eye contact for some time, not saying anything. It was Mary who eventually broke the silence. "So, what exactly do you do at work, Lucifer?"

"I work with Research and Development."

She laughed a bit, "Well, I know *that*. I *have* seen the company directory. I mean, what sort of project are you working on?"

"Oh, right," he said, his face reddening. "I'm one of the senior programmers for the human models. I'm mainly working on their personalities, but there's more involved than that."

"That sounds exciting."

He shrugged, "I suppose. It's been kind of difficult as of late, since my ideas don't seem to be too popular."

"Well, you don't want to rock the boat," she said. "You probably need to run them by the other angels in a ... pleasant way. You know, try to get them to see the benefits of your ideas in a positive light."

"Yeah, I just don't appear to be that great in that area."

They sat in silence for a moment, Lucifer taking a drink of wine and Mary really considering what was said. She then added, "Maybe you can get someone from Marketing to help you out."

Lucifer inhaled his wine and started choking on the large gulp. He began coughing, grabbing his napkin and covering his mouth as he did so. The coughing fit subsiding, he wiped the tears from his eyes, saying, "Sorry ... but, yes, angels from Marketing would probably be very ... helpful in that area."

He put down the napkin, adding, "Unfortunately, Marketing and I don't have the best relationship as of late."

"Oh," Mary simply said.

She reached for a bun in the basket on their table. Breaking it open, she began to butter it and put a piece into her mouth. As she started chewing, Lucifer asked, "What about you? What's it like being God's secretary?"

She covered her mouth with her hand as she chewed, looking up at the ceiling as she did so. "Oh, sorry," Lucifer said, realizing how impeccable his timing was.

Swallowing the food, she answered, "Between you and me, it's far from exciting. To be honest, I'm not even sure He needs a secretary."

He raised his eyebrows; she went on, "Really, hardly anyone ever comes up to visit Him, and when they do, He's ready for them. He gives me a schedule and everything, but all I really do is tell people that they can walk right in."

He chuckled, "Which is why you're normally busy with your crossword puzzles when I walk by."

Mary laughed. She looked down at the empty plate in front of her. Grabbing her fork, she began lightly tapping at the dish, deep in thought, "I'm starting to think He has me up there only for ... appearances."

They both silently considered this, staring at their plates. Mary looked back up at him, "But, you didn't really answer me when I asked what *you* do."

He grew confused. "What do you mean? I'm working on human—"

"I believe you, Lucifer," she cut him off.

He didn't know what to say.

After a brief pause, she went on, "But there must be more to it. I mean, not just *anyone* goes up to see God. Other than you, it's only really managers of the different departments I see up there."

He hadn't ever really considered it before.

She added, "And it's different with them than it is with you. They seem to come up just to give progress reports and things like that. You seem to almost come and go as you please."

He thought about it. "I guess so..."

"Of course, that hasn't been until recently, but you know what I'm trying to say."

"Yeah, I suppose." He thought about it for some time, pressing down on the prongs of his fork, raising the handle off the table as he did so. Eventually, he said, "I don't really know what to tell you. God has me doing a sort of special project." He looked at her eagerly. "If all goes as planned, I'm supposed to get a new position." His face relaxed, and he finished his thought, "But right now, I'm just another regular angel."

She nodded.

At that moment, their appetizer arrived. Samuel placed the dish that held the food in the middle of the table and gave a little flutter with his hand, saying, "*Bon appétit.*" He then backed up with a bow of his head, turned, and walked away.

The two of them were alone again. Lucifer added, "And the project's not going so well, either."

"Well, stick with it. I'm sure you'll figure it out."

Lucifer nodded, but his attention quickly turned to the carpaccio. Quite excited to try it, he spooned a piece of the thinly sliced veal onto his plate and ensured several capers and a large slice of parmesan came along. Mary followed suit, and they both put hearty portions into their own mouths. Chewing deliberately and considering the flavors they experienced, both Mary and Lucifer raised their eyebrows almost simultaneously.

Not waiting to finish chewing, Lucifer enthusiastically said, "This is really good."

With food still in her mouth as well, Mary nodded approvingly, "Yes, I'd have to agree. This was definitely a good choice."

Suddenly, both angels realized the grievous social faux pas they had committed. They simultaneously stopped the motion of their jaws and raised their hands to their own mouths, both pairs of eyes opening wide with the realization. Quite embarrassed, Lucifer took the time to actually look at Mary and saw the full-cheeked, wide-eyed, hand-on-mouth gaze coming right back at him; he felt a large smile grow on his face. Witnessing the same sight at the same time, a grin found its way to Mary's face as well. They both laughed.

Lucifer had planned out a lovely walk after dinner through a nearby park, after which they would spend some more quality time in a wine bar before the close of the night. They made their way to the park, but fate had something different in store for them. Passing by a nightclub, the music came out to greet them in the street.

Mary's excitement suddenly grew; she said, "Oh, I love this song. Lucifer, let's stop in here and dance."

Lucifer, not being much of a dancer, was a bit apprehensive at the request, but her enthusiasm made it hard to say no. They went inside.

The place was packed with angels, which made Lucifer feel even more unsure of himself. He would have preferred to have a nice, quiet evening where he could get to know Mary better, but living with that type of mindset hadn't helped him meet any angels up to this point in his life. Realizing that this could be the reason he was still alone in this world, Lucifer made it his mission to get out of his shell and to start enjoying himself as much as she was.

From the looks of things, that wasn't going to be easy, not just because Lucifer felt so out of place, but because Mary was having a great time already. She ran up a bit ahead of him and ordered some drinks. By the time he caught up to her, she had them in hand, giving one to him. They stood by the bar for a bit, taking in the scenery. The club itself wasn't extremely large, but the owner made great use of the space. The bar was out of the way, to ensure the flow of drinkers didn't get in the way of the dance floor. It looked like there was plenty of space on the balcony, overlooking the dance floor, to sit and have an enjoyable drink. Or at least there would have been lots of room up there had the club not been so full of patrons.

Mary yelled something to Lucifer, but he couldn't hear it. He yelled back, "What was that?"

"I said, 'Let's dance!'" she repeated herself.

They each took another large sip of their drinks, and then made their way to the dance floor. She started dancing, and he followed, at this point less concerned about embarrassing himself. He started off slowly, but then began giving in to the music more and more. He let go of his worries and fears and started focusing on the sounds and the sights, lights of different colors and shapes everywhere he looked.

He danced with her for a long while but did not realize how long it was; he lost all sense of time. They stopped from time to time only to order more drinks, then returned to their dancing immediately. He flowed with the music, and his head was swimming. For the first time he could remember, he was actually carefree.

Several drinks down the line, Lucifer found himself focusing less on the lights and less on the music, and more on Mary. She swayed with the beat seductively, her breasts bouncing as she did so. He watched as she twirled fluidly and became one with the music. She beckoned to him with her movements, and he began to move with her. The sights, the sounds, and the two of them all came together for one glorious moment. He embraced her; they shared a kiss.

Chapter 8

A Time for Love

Raphael walked into the office, where Lucifer was already hard at work. He stood there for some time waiting for Lucifer to look up. Lucifer gave him no acknowledgement; he wrote away, then checked his notes, followed by more writing. Raphael couldn't take it anymore; he cleared his throat.

Without looking up, Lucifer asked, "Is there something I can help you with, Raphael?"

Raphael stood there flabbergasted. Not knowing what to say or to do, he started walking toward his desk. He grabbed his chair and pulled it out, but changed his mind and pushed it back in. Turning back to Lucifer, he opened his mouth in order to say something, but nothing came out. He finally found the words he was looking for. "How can you just sit there working at a time like this? This is big! You need to tell me everything."

There was a pause as Raphael waited for Lucifer to reply. Lucifer stopped writing and thought about it for a moment. Still not facing Raphael, he eventually said, "I don't know what you're talking about." After the comment, Lucifer went back to his writing.

Raphael shook his head, quietly muttering, "You don't know what I'm talking about." This would not do. Raphael raised his eyebrows and returned to his normal speaking volume, "You know, your *date?* The first date you've been on since ... either of us could remember? That ring any bells?" Raphael chuckled a bit.

Lucifer put down his pen and turned toward Raphael. Looking Raphael square in the eyes very seriously, Lucifer told him, "I'd rather not talk about it."

Raphael put his hand over his mouth and took a step backward, "Ooh ... that bad?"

"No," Lucifer responded immediately, "I didn't say that." He picked up his pen and began to look over what he had just written before adding, "I just don't want to talk about it."

"Why not?" Raphael asked, confusion in his voice.

Lucifer didn't take the time to finish what he was reading before dropping his pen once more and turning back to Raphael, "Because, frankly, it's none of your business."

"None of my business?" Raphael laughed. Seeing Lucifer still wearing the serious face, he added, "Lucifer, don't do that."

"Why not?"

Raphael briefly collected his thoughts before continuing. It bothered him greatly that Lucifer didn't want to spill the beans, but he had to be diplomatic about the situation. "Because I took you shopping," he said.

"Right," Lucifer replied.

"And I gave you — hopefully superb — fashion advice, right?" Raphael continued.

"That is true."

"And I was the one who told you about the restaurant," Raphael said.

"You are completely correct," responded Lucifer, still not appearing to have been swayed by Raphael's words in the slightest.

"I'm even the angel who talked you into going when you were having second thoughts."

Lucifer nodded.

Raphael paused before adding, "So how can you tell me it's none of my business? Don't you think I deserve to know ... just a little bit?"

Silence. Raphael stood staring at Lucifer, both of them considering what was said.

Calmly, Raphael continued, "I mean, you can at least tell me how it went. I want to know that my suggestions ... worked out."

Lucifer pondered this. "I see your point. But, Raphael..." He paused, observing Raphael's facial expression very intently as he did so. "A good angel doesn't kiss and tell."

Raphael's eyes widened. "*Oh,* so you *kissed* her?"

Lucifer raised his hands and quickly said, "There you go, I've said too much already."

Raphael said nothing.

Lucifer looked up at him, and they shared a large smile. "The date went really well, to tell you the truth," Lucifer said. "We really hit it off." He stopped speaking, his eyes moving away from Raphael's. Lucifer slowly added, "I had a great time."

Raphael still said nothing, standing there with the smile plastered on his face.

"And that's all I'm going to say," Lucifer continued, pointing at Raphael as he did so. "Now, if you don't mind, I'd like to finish what I'm doing." Lucifer checked his watch. "I have to do a demonstration very shortly, and I'd like to be prepared."

Raphael nodded and sat down. He pulled out some papers and began to work, finally saying, "I'm just so happy for you."

Lucifer gave him no acknowledgement.

Lucifer tapped his pen on his notepad. Stopping, he stared at his blank page. He had a general idea of what he was supposed to be doing, but he had a hard time bringing himself to do it. Every time he started to focus, his mind wandered back to Mary. This kept happening in the days following their date. At first he was productive, but the more time that passed without seeing her, the more she came to mind; no matter how hard he tried, he couldn't get her out of his head.

Looking up at the clock on the office wall, Lucifer could not believe how little it had budged since the last time he checked. He looked back down at his notes that weren't quite there yet. He started visualizing a human, and he could almost see the letters materializing on the page before him, guiding his pen, but they slowly transformed into Mary's face. Mary's dark hair fell in front of her eyes, but she quickly jerked her head to the side. The hair falling back, she grabbed it with her hand, positioning it behind her ear, her eyes closed as she did so. Her face now exposed, she immediately opened her eyes, the deep blue of her iris thinly surrounding her large black pupils.

No! Stop! Focus! he thought, springing back to life as he did so.

Lucifer looked back down at his notepad, which was now adorned by a loose scribble, unidentifiable to the average passerby, that he knew was an amateur rendition of Mary's face. Seeing it as such brought him immediately back into his daydream, and the rest of the day was par for the course.

It wasn't until several hours had passed when Lucifer finally came to the conclusion that he wasn't making a great use of his time. As such, it would probably be a great idea to ask Mary out on another date; if that didn't get him on track, he wasn't really sure what would. Lucifer meandered his way over to the elevator and pressed the button for the ninety-sixth floor, the whole while thinking, *I sure am earning that paycheck today.*

Ding! The elevator doors opened, and out stepped Lucifer. He quietly wandered up to Mary's desk without her noticing; Mary was once again concentrating intently on a crossword puzzle. Lucifer leaned on the desk and cleared his throat audibly. Hearing this, she looked up at him, a large smile quickly forming on her face.

She was about to say something, but Lucifer beat her to it. "Why, hello there. I was hoping that the prettiest angel in Heaven would be able to take a bit of time out of her busy schedule to speak to me for a few minutes, but I see that God has you working far too hard. Don't worry, I won't bother you."

"Well, luckily for you," she replied, "I may be about due for a little break, and I might be able to pencil you in if you want to speak with me. However, I don't know if I'm able to fulfill your request."

"What do you mean?"

"I'm far from Heaven's prettiest angel."

"Come on," Lucifer responded right away, "that's a lie, and you know it."

"Oh, stop," she said, waving her hand as she did so. "What can I do for you, Lucifer?"

"Well ... I was thinking..."

She raised her eyebrows. "And...?"

Lucifer continued what he was saying, "...and I think ... that our previous ... engagement went really well. I mean, I had a great time, and you ... seemed to ... as well?"

She nodded, still smiling.

He shrugged, "Well, if we both had such a great time, I think it would be ... unfortunate ... to leave it at just one outing together. I mean, think of all the fun we would be missing out on, and I think that would be just ... tragic."

She laughed. "I guess you're right, and I don't think it's fair to bestow such tragedy upon you. What did you have in mind, Lucifer?"

"Well, to be honest," he answered, "I hadn't really thought about it much. But I'm pretty creative, I think. If you give me a bit of time, I think I can come up with some wonderfully romantic way to spend our time. Say—" He stopped to consider it before continuing, "tomorrow night?"

"Tomorrow night's no good for me, unfortunately. I've got my book club."

He stepped back slightly out of surprise. "You go to a book club?"

She frowned at his reaction. Now with slight irritation in her voice, she responded, "Why, do I not seem like the type of angel who would read?"

"No, it's not that. I'm just ... learning more and more about you all the time."

"Well, I'm free the next day. If the creative Lucifer can come up with something wonderfully romantic for us to do, I'm sure I can teach him all about me."

Learning more about Mary being exactly what Lucifer wanted, he ensured he came up with a wonderfully romantic outing. Shortly before their date, Lucifer took a trip over to the grocery store to pick up some supplies. As he was perusing the aisles, he saw a familiar face.

"Zack!" Lucifer said upon recognition.

Isaac looked up and immediately gave a large smile, "Why, if it isn't my cheese-loving friend." Isaac briefly glanced at the items in Lucifer's basket before adding, "Still indulging, I see. How's your life treating you?"

Lucifer shared the smile with Isaac. "You know, it's great. I think last time I saw you, I was really struggling ... swimming upstream. But I took your advice and made the best of the situation, and everything's looking up. My job's going better, I'm seeing the best angel ever, the apple of my eye — life is good."

Isaac kept smiling big, showing off all his teeth. He nodded slightly as he said, "That's great."

Lucifer's smile slowly dissolved off of his face. He really couldn't put his finger on it, but something about Isaac's tone seemed almost forced.

With no response from Lucifer, Isaac eventually added, "Well, I'm just going on lunch, so I can't stay and chat right now. But, it's been really good seeing you."

Lucifer offered his hand to Isaac. "My name's Lucifer, by the way."

Isaac shook his hand, saying, "Lucifer ... that's not a very common name. Please forgive me if I don't remember it."

"Don't worry, Zack," Lucifer replied, "I wouldn't dream of holding it against you."

With that, they parted. As Isaac walked away, Lucifer could hear him muttering to himself, "Lucifer ... Lucifer..."

Lucifer picked up Mary for their date, and they biked over to the lovely High Cloud Park. He remembered a quite romantic spot in the shade of an apple tree that gave a majestic view of all the heavens. Arriving there, it was better than he could have imagined: Not only was it a clear day, providing an unobscured view of all that surrounded them and the sky above, but also the apple blossoms were in full bloom. The sight was breathtaking, with the deep blue of the sky as far as the eye could see and the sun's rays playing off the greens of the grassy meadow below and the yellows of the flowers that filled it. It all mixed with the bright pinks of the apple blossoms, some releasing their tight grips on the branches to float through the sky in the gentle breeze. Far below them was the city, a spectacular sight in its own right, miniscule as it was from their vantage point. The cityscape, in its epic God-made splendor, greatly contrasted the more natural God-made countryside.

They approached the spot, and Mary was blown away.

"Wow," she said, coming to a stop just outside the shadow cast by the tree. "How did you ever find this place?"

Lucifer laid his bicycle in the field and wandered into the shade with a basket. "I don't know," he answered. "I've been coming here since..." He turned to face her, finishing his thought, "as long as I can remember."

She merely nodded and stayed where she was, holding her bicycle and continuing to take in the majestic view.

Lucifer opened the basket, bringing forth a large, checkered blanket, flapping it out and laying it across the ground. "I used to come here all the time." Lucifer was crouching as he spoke, flattening out the blanket over the grass. He paused and looked back to her, a twinkle in his eye as he went on, "I would always come right here, to this apple tree. I'd usually bring a good book and read and read for hours on end."

He looked out at the city, continuing, "Sometimes I'd just lay in the shade, letting my thoughts wander ... feeling my eyelids slowly grow heavy..." He smiled, "Then I'd realize I just fell asleep."

He chuckled quietly to himself. They both remained where they were in silent contentment for a moment, enjoying the beauty all around them. Lucifer then put the basket down on the blanket and stood up, turning back to Mary. "Of course," he added, "that was before the project."

He walked closer to her. She slowly lowered her bike to the ground then approached him, taking his outstretched hand.

As Lucifer led her to the blanket, he finished his thought with a sigh. “Life was much simpler then.”

They both sat on the blanket. Lucifer opened the basket once more, and Mary excitedly asked, “So what types of goodies did you bring on this excursion?”

“Why, only the best for you, my dear,” he responded, revealing the contents of the basket as he spoke. “I figured we could start off with some lovely *cretons* to be spread upon this light baguette.”

Seeing a look of confusion as she looked upon the container with the *cretons,* Lucifer quickly added, “In case you were wondering, it’s basically ground pork with spices.” He considered what he just said before adding, “Believe me, it’s much better than I’m making it sound right now.”

Reaching back into the basket, Lucifer brought forth more food. “Some delectable Camembert cheese, along with some crackers. He rummaged as he spoke. “Here are some ciabatta buns along with prosciutto, salami, and anything else you may need for sandwich making — mustard, pickles, you name it. Some grapes and sliced melon, which, I may add, makes a great combination with prosciutto, if you so desire.

“And...” Lucifer paused for effect as he made sure he had a good grip on the remnants of the basket. “Champagne?”

To his surprise, Mary’s excitement quickly faded. Looking down, he could see why. In one hand, he held the bottle of champagne; in the other, he clutched the bases of two champagne glasses, broken immediately above the stems.

Mary laughed, “Would it be largely unromantic if we were to drink from the bottle?”

As the evening went by, the clear sky began filling up with clouds. The sun started to set, and the blue of the sky slowly transformed into brilliant yellows and reds.

"Lucifer," Mary quietly said, laying on her back on top of the blanket, "you brought so much food. I can't believe we ate that much."

Sitting up next to her, Lucifer was in the middle of taking a large gulp of champagne straight from the bottle. Finishing, he brought the bottle down, wiping his mouth as he did so. "Yeah, I know," he replied. "It was all so good, I couldn't stop until I had a bit of everything."

With that, he passed the bottle to her. Seeing it in her periphery, Mary turned her gaze toward it. She shifted onto her side, taking the champagne and drinking from the bottle.

As she finished, Lucifer asked, "So, was this date to your liking?"

"Well, the night's still young," she responded with a sly grin.

"I know, but I'm just inquiring as to whether or not the romance was at, you know ... an acceptable level."

She smiled, saying, "Lucifer, it's been a perfect date ... wonderfully romantic."

He added, "Romantic enough for you to teach me all about yourself?"

She laughed, "Ah, yes, I forgot all about that. What did you want to know, Lucifer?"

With that she passed the bottle back to him. He took it, asking, "What would I *not* want to know? I'd love to hear all about you."

"Ask me anything."

"Anything, eh?" He said, drinking some more champagne while he thought about it. "Okay, I guess we can start out with something easy ... What's your favorite food?"

She scrunched her mouth together as she considered it, "I'd have to say I'm a pasta fan. I could probably eat spaghetti every meal of every day and never get sick of it, so I'm going to say that."

He nodded and asked, "How about music? You seemed to like the stuff in that club the other night."

"Well, yes," she answered. "I pretty much like most music ... as long as it isn't country."

He laughed a bit before continuing, "Favorite color?"

"I've always had a little spot in my heart for pink."

He opened his mouth, but she added, "And not just any pink. It's almost like a fluorescent pink, with a bit of an orange tinge to it."

Lucifer smiled, saying, "How specific of you."

Mary laughed. "How about you? You don't strike me as a pink lover."

Lucifer's eyebrows went up and he shrugged, "My favorite color? I never really thought about it much ... Red, I guess, but I'm not really that particular."

She nodded; he went on, "Out of curiosity more than anything, what book were you reading for your book club?"

She snickered quietly, "Oh, nothing exciting. The book's called *Life Is Beautiful,* and it's the typical type of thing we read. You know, very lovely imagery, some large romantic happenstance..."

He smiled at the picture she was painting.

Mary added, "...sterile plot, more boring than you can imagine."

Lucifer laughed. She continued, "I don't know, I think a better story needs something ... to happen. Some sort of hardship ... some tragedy, even if it's almost negligible. But, that's the problem with the novels the other angels want to read; everyone just wants to be sheltered from that sort of thing, to not even think about it."

"I know what you mean ... more than you know," Lucifer said, the smile slowly leaving his face. "But the one thing I don't understand is why do you keep going to the book club if you don't like the books?"

She shrugged, "I guess it's more for the social aspect; I'll gladly read through a book like that if it means I have an excuse to get out with my friends more often."

They looked away from each other, nodding silently for a moment. A smirk came to Lucifer's face, and he went on with his questioning with excitement in his voice. "Oh, do you do crosswords only, or do you ever try out word searches?"

Mary laughed. "Actually, I was thinking of branching out and trying my luck with some Sudoku."

Lucifer looked up as he thought about another question. "What about relationships? You must have gone out with a ... number of ... angels?"

"Ooh, this questioning is getting more gutsy." Mary smiled as she spoke. "What makes you say that? Because I'm 'Heaven's prettiest angel?'"

He thought about it before responding, "Well ... yeah, I guess. You're also, you know, not really that shy or anything."

"Well, it may surprise you to know that I don't really get out that much. I'll go out with some friends from time to time, but I don't really get asked out."

Satisfied with that answer, he nodded.

She frowned slightly, adding, "But what are you talking about? You're not that shy either."

He grew confused. "Sure I am."

"Well, you were pretty nervous when you came up to talk to me, but you still did it. Plus, listen to you now." She motioned for him to hand the bottle back to her as she spoke.

"That's just because I'm getting to know you," Lucifer responded, giving her the champagne. "If you saw me when I'm out of my element ... I'm timid as a mouse."

She gave him a blank stare.

"You know," he added, "those small, furry animals?"

She shook her head.

"Basically, I'm shy," he said.

"Well, that's not what I heard," Mary replied, raising her eyebrows slightly. She brought the bottle to her mouth, not taking her eyes off him as she drank.

He waited in silence for Mary to finish, perplexed by her comment. As she brought the bottle down, he continued the conversation, "What are you talking about?"

She looked to both sides of her, not that anyone was around, answering him in a lower voice. "It's not that I was eavesdropping or anything, but I heard some angels talking about you in passing."

Hearing this, Lucifer raised his eyebrows without realizing it.

Mary went on. "They seemed to think you had no problem expressing whatever was on your mind, no matter how negative the reaction is."

"What did they say?"

She smiled at him. "Let's just say I understand what you mean about the relationship between you and Marketing."

He nodded slowly.

"So, you can't tell me you're shy when I'm not around," Mary added.

"Well, I guess not ... but that's kind of a recent thing. Okay, then I *used* to be shy."

"Well, I guess you're growing as an angel," she said, taking another drink from the bottle afterwards.

He sighed.

"And besides," Mary added, "confidence is sexy."

Lucifer smiled, scooting a bit closer to her as he said, "Well, it's a good thing that I'm starting to ... exude ... confidence, then."

Mary came closer to him as well. He brought his arm around her, and she placed a palm on his chest. Their lips united in a most sensual exchange.

Chapter 9

Fixing It

Maxwell and Raphael stood in the geo-cultivation room upon one of Raphael's test landscapes, at the top of a cliff overlooking a large valley. Off in the distance, down below, a small freshwater lake found itself surrounded on all sides by a luscious forest. Behind them stood several mountains, so tall that clouds peppered their snow-covered tips. The spot in which they now stood was bare rock; the grass began around them, several feet away on all sides, excluding the face of the cliff. From there, various scatterings of trees and bushes extruded from the landscape, wherever they could fit themselves amongst the other vegetation.

Maxwell pulled down his safety goggles to protect his eyes from the ensuing wind. He stood, preparing to jot down notes on his clipboard, while Raphael knelt beside him, ready to observe every little detail. "Run Wind Program," said Maxwell.

Immediately upon the command being spoken, wind picked up, causing the trees, grass, and bushes on the test landscape to move as it did so. Maxwell jotted down a few notes before shouting, “Speed up five hundred thousand percent.”

The movements of the landscape picked up, appearing very jerky with the increased speed. Over the course of a few seconds, the light began to fade, and night fell on the landscape. After waiting several seconds for night to become day once more, Maxwell audibly said, “Fix light to this illumination.”

The words spoken, the light no longer faded from the landscape. Raphael looked up at Maxwell, saying, “Okay, let’s get things moving. Speed up two million percent.”

The vegetation no longer moved; it changed so quickly that it appeared before them as distinct snapshots at different points in time. Only now did the changes to the landscape become noticeable; the rock face of the cliff began to recede as pieces fell off, the falling happening so fast that it looked as though the pieces more or less disappeared. Almost immediately, Raphael loudly said, “Pause program.”

The wind stopped and the landscape remained as it was when the command was given, branches of trees twisted this way and that. Maxwell stopped writing. Putting his pen on the clipboard, he asked, “Why’d you do that?”

Raphael waited to answer him, staring at the frozen landscape. He eventually looked back up at Maxwell, saying, “Because it’s not right.”

Lowering his notes, and with annoyance in his voice, Maxwell added, “What are you talking about? We just started the test. Shouldn’t we wait a bit more? You know, take a few notes?”

“Why would we keep going if it’s already wrong?”

Raphael looked back toward the edge of the cliff after the comment. Maxwell merely looked back at him, not adding anything to the conversation. Raphael stood up and walked forward slightly, saying, “See there, about ten meters ahead?”

He walked closer, pointing at the spot his gaze was fixed upon. He kept going, now looking back at Maxwell to ensure he was paying attention. Raphael stopped moving, his index finger aiming at the ground directly in front of him.

Maxwell said, "What about it?"

"Look at the indentation," Raphael elaborated.

Maxwell stepped a bit closer, trying to examine the rock to which Raphael was referring. He shook his head. "I can't say I know what you're talking about."

Raphael was shocked at Maxwell's attention to detail, or lack thereof. He explained, "Look at how deep the indentation is becoming in this one spot." Seeing no reaction from Maxwell, he continued, "We need to excise more control over the program. This may not look like much now, but unchecked, this is liable to completely destroy everything."

With a large groan, Maxwell retorted, "You're overreacting, Raphael. I'm sure this won't turn out as bad as you're saying."

Raphael's eyebrows went up, "Oh yeah? Un-pause!"

With that, the landscape came back to life, and they continued to watch the choppy snapshots. Slowly, even at the great speed, the indentation grew until it became a great chasm. Both angels stepped back slightly as it came close to their feet. Eventually, the rocks began to crumble and topple into the center of it, the pile gradually growing and growing.

"Pause program."

The words came from the lips of Maxwell this time. They stood in silent thought for a moment, merely observing the once mighty cliff now sitting before them as a pile of rubble. Maxwell brought his pen to his mouth as he considered it, walking closer to the rubble, stopping and looking down at it. He eventually said, "Okay, you're right."

Raphael glanced up from the disappointing ruin before him back to Maxwell, who then continued, "But what can we do about it?"

Raphael clapped his hands once. Bringing his index finger toward Maxwell, he said, "I have an idea." Much louder, he quickly added, "Reset to year zero."

The rubble and chasm disappeared, and the landscape reverted back to the way it once looked. Raphael shook his finger as he went on with his thought, "We obviously need to alter some parameters."

Before Maxwell could add anything to the discussion, Raphael quickly spun around, walking closer to the cliff's edge as he spoke. "Make an adjustment to distribute the wind more evenly along the facc and focus less force on this one spot. That should create less of a sharp crevasse and more of a smooth, longer indent. It shouldn't cause such a drastic effect."

"Okay," replied Maxwell as he scribbled furiously upon his clipboard, "there, let's give it a try. Run program."

The wind picked up once more, and both angels turned their focus back to the landscape, Raphael crouching once again. Hardly any time passed when Raphael stood up quickly and spoke. "No, no, no! Pause program!"

Everything froze. Wearing a dumbfounded look, Maxwell turned to Raphael. Growing noticeably annoyed, Maxwell asked, "Well? What is it this time?"

Raphael merely stood with his hand on his chin, shaking his head.

Maxwell brought both hands down, one of them still clutching his clipboard. He shouted, "I can see that the distribution is more even this time! What seems to be the problem?"

"We're heading for the same end result," Raphael answered much more calmly.

"Can't we watch it a bit longer to see for sure? I'd like to take some better notes to really know how well the adjustments work."

Raphael kept shaking his head silently. After a few seconds, he quietly said, "Fine."

Maxwell nodded his head knowingly, saying, “Okay, then. Un-pause.”

With that, the landscape came alive once more. Both angels continued their observation, Maxwell making notes as he did so, and Raphael silently staring. The wind slowly wore away at the cliff, creating a smoother curve this time. However, two points around the location of the previous indentation were breaking away more quickly than the center, the result of which was two separate openings. Both grew and grew, but the rock in the middle continued to stand tall and proud, the wind circling around, wearing down the stone surrounding the resulting spire more and more as it did so.

Seeing the interesting formation come into being, Maxwell raised his eyebrows and nodded approvingly. Turning his gaze to Raphael briefly, he saw that Raphael continued his head shaking and chin holding. Maxwell brought his attention back to his notes and the changing face of the cliff. The opening around the spire grew and grew, smaller rocks settling all around it. While much girth remained near the top of the structure, the base became worn down to the point of being unable to support the top any longer. Suddenly, the spire toppled under its own size and weight, collapsing down into the center of the clearing. To the angels, it happened so fast that it was standing there one second, gone the next. The force with which it fell caused it to break into pieces, some large and many quite small, bringing the familiar end result of a hole containing a pile of rubble.

Maxwell was once again at a loss for words.

With the program still running, Raphael stepped closer to him, shouting over the gusting wind, “Now are you happy?”

Maxwell was puzzled, and it showed on his face. Raphael folded his arms over his chest, turning to kick a rock into the hole. Almost as though someone threw a switch on in his head, Maxwell’s face suddenly lit up. Scribbling on his notes, he announced, “It seems that I have had something of an epiphany.”

Raphael turned back to face him, curiously asking, “Oh yeah? And what might that be?”

Maxwell ignored the question until he stopped writing, marking a very obvious period with a loud tap on his page. He then said with a smile, “Just watch. Reset to year zero.”

The hole immediately mended itself back to its original form, the wind continuing to blow. Raphael watched and could see the top of the cliff being worn away slowly and much more evenly than before. Both he and Maxwell stepped closer to observe the changes more intently. The edge was breaking away, but smoother gradients were being created; indentations were made, but not growing into great chasms.

Both of them nodded, pleased with the ensuing results. Raphael asked, “What did you do? It’s looking much better.”

Maxwell pointed his pen toward Raphael as he replied, “I altered the wind gusts so they are more intermittent in nature, with changing force in different areas. I also—”

His explanation was cut off as the ground began to move. Both Raphael and Maxwell were shocked to see the rocks immediately in front of them come loose and fall into the hole. Due to the increased speed at which they were observing, the fall occurred almost instantaneously, the ledge disappearing before their eyes. Acting as quickly as he could, Raphael shouted, “Pause program!”

Everything froze. Looking down, they each could see that the large rock they were standing on had begun to fall as well. Had Raphael spoke even a second later, it probably would have been smashed on the ground below. Instead, it floated two-thirds of the way down the cliff, or what remained of it.

Raphael looked to Maxwell, who only now, looking back at Raphael, finished his thought, “I also worked the majority of gusts further down the cliff, so as to not just affect the top, but the cliff as a whole."

Raphael shook his head once again, adding, "And I see it worked out well for you."

Maxwell explained, "I'm trying out different settings. Some are bound to fail, but we need to press on."

"But we're not making any progress."

Maxwell took offense to this remark. "Not making any progress? Look at what we accomplished. We found settings that make this particular landscape create a ... majestic spire, and almost sorted out your problem with chasms through the intermittent gusts."

Raphael's eyes widened and he laughed, "'Almost sorted out?' No matter what parameters we change, it always ends up as rubble."

"Well, maybe there's a lesson in that." Maxwell's tone became very somber. "Maybe none of our landscapes will last beyond a certain point."

"No," Raphael responded immediately, shaking his head, "I can't accept that. That the landscapes will not be recognizable in ten thousand years' time, that's fine. But that the world will eventually be a pile of rubble?"

"Then why don't you sketch me out a drawing for each of your landscapes at each point in time, and I'll see what I can do."

Raphael frowned, "You know that isn't a plausible solution. I don't have the time."

"And that's exactly my point," Maxwell paused to let this sink in. "Raphael, we don't have unlimited time to work on this. Look, our previous experiments have led to a similar conclusion; if everything approaches eventual destruction, we're just going to have to accept it."

"I guess that's where you and I differ," Raphael retorted. "I've spent ages designing these landscapes, and I'm not just going to send them through the Erosion machine to have them destroyed."

Maxwell shrugged, "Maybe we can leave it running, but we'll still have to go back and touch things up every fifty years or so."

"So, Erosion knocks it down, and then we set it back up? What a waste! I might as well just do what we originally suggested and maintain all my landscapes by hand."

Maxwell shouted, "You know that's not practical! You can't do that on your own, anyway. What do you think it would take to maintain things to your liking, twenty angels per mountain?"

Raphael looked away from Maxwell, saying, "No matter how painstaking it is, I'd rather see it through the right way."

"You know we don't have those kinds of resources," Maxwell added, letting out a huge sigh. "All the other angels have their own projects to look after, and if you tried to deal with it on your own, you would have to compromise quality for speed no matter how you slice it."

Maxwell turned away from Raphael as well. He gave a smaller sigh, "Come on, Raphael, you know this program is important; don't give up on it. Remember what awaits us when we finish: no constant maintenance, no touch-ups, just flicking the switch and letting it go. Raphael ... We're still making headway. We just need to work on it some more."

The loud crackle of the intercom interrupted their conversation. The voice on the other end spoke, "To the two angels occupying Geo-cultivation Room Number One: Your time is up. Please vacate to make room for the next booking."

Maxwell and Raphael looked at each other, then down to the rock, frozen in freefall, upon which they now stood. Raphael then said, "Remove landscape," at which point the test landscape faded away. The rock vanished and their feet were in fact firmly planted on the floor in middle of the large, white room. They both slowly made their way to the exit.

The two human models stood motionless in the middle of the large white room, both still with impeccable clothing and hair, their respective numbers residing in the middle of each of their chests. Lucifer stood next to them, glancing over his clipboard and the many scribbles thereupon with another angel – the same angel who had shown Lucifer the previous interaction – awaiting input.

"First of all," Lucifer began, "I just wanted to say that we're definitely making strides with the walk. Honestly, it's much more natural now, and that makes a world of a difference."

"Thanks. Yes, I took your suggestion to heart, and I couldn't agree with you more," the angel said.

"However," Lucifer began speaking, but paused to fully express the importance of what he was about to say. He brought his hand forward and aimed it directly at the other angel before continuing, "I would like to talk to you about the rest of their personalities."

Confusion on the angel's face, he asked, "What, exactly, do you mean?"

Lucifer put his hand down. He went on, nonchalantly, "I mean exactly what I said." Pausing once more, he turned to face the humans, "I'm talking about their behavior ... their gestures..."

Moving toward the models, he began using finger quotes for emphasis as he spoke, "...their 'feelings' ... their 'emotions' ... their 'reason'..."

Turning back to the angel, he continued, "You know, everything that makes up their personality."

The angel looked at the models and then back to Lucifer. "I ... still can't say that I'm following you."

"Can I ask you something?" inquired Lucifer. "What is our project? What are we doing here?"

"Um ... well, we're creating man, the Earth, the universe ... everything."

"Yes," Lucifer went on, "but what are *we* – you and I – doing, specifically?"

"Well, right now we're sculpting a personality for man," the angel answered, pushing his sliding glasses back up his nose as he did so.

"To that, I need to say yes – and no. Yes, we are *supposed* to be sculpting this personality, and, yes, we are sculpting *a* personality..." He turned back toward the lifeless humans and slowly finished his thought, "But *this* is not the personality of a man."

They stood in silence. Lucifer looked back at the angel and saw that he was truly attempting to understand what was being said.

"Actually, I take that back," Lucifer went on. "I can see this being the personality of *a* man ... but not *all* men."

The angel nervously spoke, "To be fair, God didn't give us very much direction. All He really said was to 'create man in His image.'"

Lucifer considered that, asking, "And what does 'God's image' bring to mind?"

The angel looked to the floor, then toward his models. He thought long and hard, and then confidently stated, "Perfection."

Lucifer sighed. With an open hand aimed at the humans, he said, "Do you believe that these ... are perfection?"

"No." He looked back at Lucifer and quickly added, "But I do believe it's a start."

"I agree," Lucifer added immediately. He turned back to the other angel, slowly continuing, "But for us to be on the same page, you need to tell me what *you* are striving for. If these were to become perfect, what would that be? What would that *look* like? What would that *act* like?"

"I suppose ... it would be intelligent beings ... who are very civil ... with a strong moral center." The angel nodded. His eyes lighting up, he looked to Lucifer, adding, "Everyone looking out for one another, no inequality. It would cause great pain to act thoughtlessly."

Lucifer nodded back. He went on, "Okay, with that being said: If everything is perfect, what would be the point in living?" Lucifer looked through the other angel, past him. He repeated his comment in a whisper, "What would be the point in living?"

He looked back at the other angel's face and could see only confusion. Lucifer spoke much louder, clenching a fist and driving it down through the air as he drove home each point. "*What* would be the point in *living?* Where would there be a *drive* to do better? How do you expect humans to *learn* and to *grow...*" Turning to the humans, Lucifer finished his thought with a whisper, "If they're already perfect?"

The other angel said nothing.

Turning back toward him, Lucifer continued in a normal speaking voice, "Don't you think that a little hardship could turn what I'm proposing to you to be an apathetic society into one full of ambition?"

They both stood in silence, processing the words in their minds. They looked at the humans, Human #2 frozen with a smile on his face as he clutched his gift, the apple, presented to him by Human #1 at the end of the interaction. Both angels fixed their gazes on the lifeless expression on each human's face; the models stared at nothing, and neither appeared capable of understanding anything about the world around them.

The other angel turned to Lucifer, saying, "May I ask you a question, then?"

"Of course," Lucifer nodded.

"Just so we *are* on the same page ... what are *you* striving for? How do you want humans to turn out?"

Continuing to look at the models, Lucifer answered, "I see them to be the same as you see — but I also see the opposite." He looked back at the angel and walked closer to him, "I see caring, thoughtful individuals, but I also see amoral, selfish humans walking among them.

"I see apathetic individuals with no drive to do anything more than provide themselves with sustenance and expend as little energy as possible, and those with so much ambition that they can hardly contain it in their beings. I see humans who are so beautiful that simply gazing at them will make a tear come to your eye, and those who are the very definition of repulsive, along with everything in between."

The angel stood there in awe, not even noticing his glasses slip down his nose.

Lucifer went on. "I see the most diverse group of individuals you could dream of. I see — actually, are you familiar with any of the work being done on snow and snowflakes?"

"Vaguely," the angel replied.

"You really should look into it sometime. Anyway, the angels doing this work have perfected a program that generates the shapes of the snowflakes, very intricate if you look up close. The interesting thing about this program is that it can generate so many novel designs for the snowflakes that the probability of actually finding two that have an identical shape is something in the realm of one in nine hundred trillion. And, yet, they never lose their similarities. You would never look at one and question that it is a snowflake."

He paused to allow the angel to process this information before getting to the point. "The current human physiology can allow for an amazing array of diversity, such as I described. All we need is a program that implements it; you know, giving each human a completely different personality at its creation. I propose we approach these angels, the snowflake angels, and see if they would allow us to adapt their program for our uses, for human personalities."

The angel shrugged, "You know, you may be right. It could be worth a try."

Lucifer smiled. After looking the other angel up and down, he said, "You know, all this time we've been working together, and I don't believe I ever caught your name."

"Oh, it's Charles."

"Lucifer," Lucifer said, offering his hand to Charles.

"Yes," Charles replied, taking Lucifer's hand and shaking it. "I know."

"Well, let this be our official introduction. We'll start things off again on the right foot."

Still shaking Charles's hand, Lucifer brought up the index finger of his opposite hand and continued, "And don't be shy. If you ever have any ideas – or concerns – feel free to talk to me any time."

Charles released Lucifer's hand, chuckling, "It sounds like you had a lot of time to think about this. Why didn't you make these suggestions long ago? Now I've spent so long pursuing the wrong path."

Lucifer considered it. "I suppose ... I didn't know how."

They both nodded in silence.

"But never fear," Lucifer went on, "it's never too late to fix things."

At that very moment, they heard the loud crackle of the intercom turning on. "Hello, my fellow angels. This is Michael speaking to you with excellent news. After meeting with God and the other department managers, we are pleased to announce that the project has been given a release date. We will be unveiling in exactly two weeks' time."

Both Lucifer's and Charles's jaws dropped. Lucifer's hands temporarily stopped working, and his grip loosened on his clipboard, causing it to fall to the ground with an audible crash followed by the quieter sound of his pen coming loose from the clipboard and rolling across the floor.

Michael continued, "Now, we do realize that the next two weeks will be hard work and much more stressful than usual, but the project is moving along at an *exceptional* pace, and we believe in all of you, the dedicated workers. So, be proud, stay strong, and we will surely turn out something for the ages."

The intercom went off with a loud clack. Lucifer and Charles merely stood in the middle of the large room in silent shock.

Lucifer nervously fidgeted in the elevator as he approached the top floor of the building. All of the angels he passed in the short walk from R&D's model testing room to the elevator appeared overjoyed at the announcement, which led him to believe that the ensuing conversation was going to be much more difficult than he had initially anticipated. That was truly saying a lot, as he had initially anticipated spectacular failure.

Ding! The elevator doors opened, and out came a twitchy Lucifer, touching his fingertips together repeatedly and grinding his teeth subconsciously as he walked. Mary noticed him immediately and greeted him with a large smile. "Why, hello there."

He turned his glance toward Mary and flashed her a quick smile that almost immediately dropped off his face in a frown, at which point he continued his catastrophizing.

She easily caught wind of the situation. "Lucifer ... are you all right? You look terrible."

He approached the front of her desk and stopped. Looking himself up and down, he responded, "Really? Oh, I suppose you're right. I'm a mess. But it's not my fault; I think it's fair to be a mess when *someone* is actively ruining everything I'm striving toward."

His angry tone startled her, and he could see that. He calmed his voice, leaning on her desk and rubbing his eyes with his thumb and index finger as he did so. "I'm sorry, Mary. I don't want you to think that I'm mad at you or anything. I'm just frustrated, that's all." He perked up suddenly. "But I'm going to try and deal with it right now, and we'll see how that goes."

"Oh, but you can't—"

"Wish me luck," he interrupted, walking toward God's open door.

"Lucifer, I don't think—"

"Oh, and I just wanted to tell you that I really care about you, Mary," speaking quickly, he cut her off once more, stopping in front of the desk again. He then spoke more slowly, "I mean it, and I just wanted to make sure you know that, you know, in case I forget to mention it ... later on."

She smiled. "Aw, Lucifer. That really means a lot to me."

"We definitely have to get together again sometime soon," he added. "But for now, duty calls."

He started toward the office once more with a much faster stride. Mary reached out toward him, fingers extended, and quickly said, "No, Lucifer, He's in there with someone right now."

It was too late; he was already through the doorway. God and Gabriel sat staring at Lucifer, looking as though they were in the middle of a conversation that was abruptly cut short. Lucifer merely said, "Ooh..."

All three remained where they were, frozen in silence. Lucifer could faintly hear Mary whispering to him, "I tried to tell you."

Lucifer was the first in the room to speak, "I'm sorry. You two finish up and ... I'll just be out here."

God put His hand forward. "Oh no, by all means, I will talk to you now. I know it's important."

He turned to Gabriel. "Let us meet tomorrow at ten o'clock, and we will finish up then. How does that sound?"

Gabriel looked at Lucifer, then back to the Lord, saying, "No problem. I will see You then."

With that, Gabriel gathered his things and got up. He walked past Lucifer, staring the whole time he moved. Lucifer could see the confusion on Gabriel's face; it was almost as if he spoke without speaking. "Why is your time with God more important than mine?" Gabriel's look asked Lucifer. Lucifer gave him no response.

Gabriel gone, Lucifer immediately snapped back into action. He looked to God and pointed at the door, asking, "Do You mind?"

"If that is your wish."

Lucifer closed the door and walked into the room. God motioned toward a chair, and Lucifer sat. They both composed themselves, and God decided to break the ice. "So, Lucifer, what's on your mind?"

"Do You even have to ask that question?" Lucifer said with annoyance in his voice.

God looked confused.

"No, cut that out," Lucifer continued. "You knew I was going to say that."

A frown came to God's face, and He lowered His eyebrows. "What do you want Me to do, Lucifer, have a conversation with Myself?" he asked. "We both know you wouldn't want that, so let's not play this game."

Lucifer gave Him a pleading look and gently said, "This isn't a game. Why don't You tell me what's on my mind?"

There was no response.

Lucifer quietly added, "Please?"

God sat in silence momentarily. He then nodded, saying, "Very well, Lucifer ... you think that I have made a mistake."

They sat in silence once more while Lucifer collected his thoughts. He quietly asked, "Well ... haven't You?"

"No." God did not hesitate.

"Do You seriously think the project will be at a point of completion in two weeks' time?" Lucifer asked in a much harsher tone.

"No, Lucifer, I don't *think* it will be at a point of completion — I *know* it will."

Lucifer sighed, "Then I suppose it will be proper to assume that there would be nothing I could do to talk You into pushing the release date back."

"That would be a safe assumption."

Before Lucifer could say anything else, God went on, speaking quickly, "And I'll even go so far as to save you the trouble of asking Me why this is the case. Since telling you that I know, for a fact, that it will be finished — to My liking — in two weeks' time would not be a sufficient answer for you, I can also assure you that the department managers and I went through the numbers and all agreed that two weeks would be more than sufficient."

Lucifer opened his mouth, but God put up His hand and continued, "However, I am aware that you do not trust that your idea of complete and the department managers' ideas of complete are even close to the same pattern of thought, so this would not be a good enough answer for you. In that case, I would remind you of all the excitement you witnessed on the way to the elevator. Consider how much of a crushing blow it would be to the morale of every single angel in this building if I were to tell them that, no, I do not, in fact, believe that it can be done in that timeframe — that I no longer believe in their abilities or believe in *them*. How do you think they would react?

"No, Lucifer, there is no changing this. All I can tell you is that you need to have a little faith."

They sat in silence. Lucifer felt the heavy weight of defeat pressing down on him once more. God remained patient as Lucifer looked at the desk and studied the grains in the wood. Eventually, he looked back up at the Lord, saying, "May I ask You something?"`

God nodded. "Of course. You may ask Me anything you want."

"And will You give me an honest answer?" Lucifer continued the question, feeling that he needed to be a bit more specific if he didn't want more disappointment.

"By all means."

Lucifer tapped at the desk, looking up to the ceiling, thinking of the best way to ask his question. He slowly brought his gaze back to God, saying, "Do You know what it's like ... to be me?"

"Yes," God answered simply.

Lucifer thought about it for a moment before continuing, "But do You get the whole experience? Do You feel what I feel? Do You experience the same emotions that I do?"

God waited a moment before answering, nodding slowly, "Yes, I do."

Lucifer was becoming irritated. He had to understand, but he felt that it was impossible. "Then why are You ruining my life?" he shouted.

God frowned. With a sigh, He said, "Lucifer ... I'm not ruining your life. Sure, your life has been changing immensely over the last short while, and it has been quite a bit to take in, I know, but I'm merely giving you this opportunity to learn ... to evolve."

He paused, giving Lucifer the chance to really consider His words. God quietly added, "What you do with this time is up to you."

Lucifer stared into His eyes, "But You know what will happen."

God leaned back, "Well, Lucifer, that doesn't matter." He paused once more. God swiveled His chair, facing the painting on the wall. He then slowly turned back to Lucifer, coming to a rest facing him once more. God said, "What you and I both know is, you have a great deal of work ahead of you and sitting here is just wasting valuable time. I suggest going back down to the model testing room to start things off."

Lucifer grew confused. "Why is that?"

"Your clipboard's still sitting in the middle of the floor."

Chapter 10

A Moment's Peace

Raphael sat in his office working as hard as he could to solve the problem of the faulty Erosion program. His mind was beginning to mirror his desk, in its usual state of disarray. No matter how hard he tried, he just couldn't solve the problem; there were too many variables and no way to account for everything. No matter how they altered the parameters, even if they backed up on the force of the wind, it still became rubble later on. With enough time, Erosion made a mockery of all of his skillfully crafted landscapes. As well, if they appeared to be making headway with one landscape, any adjustments made seemed to ruin any progress they made on another one.

But he knew that Maxwell was right: Erosion was an important program. He had to trudge on and work out the bugs. It was just hard to determine how to properly approach the problem.

Raphael stopped what he was doing. He had the peculiar feeling that he was being watched. Sure enough, looking back at the doorway to the office proved him to be correct. Gabriel was observing him silently.

"Oh my gosh," Raphael said. "Gabe, how long were you standing there?"

Gabriel shrugged. "Oh ... not long."

Raphael could not be totally sure if that was the truth, as he knew Gabriel would never let him know that he had kept him waiting. "Well, why didn't you say anything?" Raphael asked.

Gabriel ran his finger up and down the door frame. "I guess ... it looked like you were deep in thought, and I didn't want to ruin your concentration. I know how it is to have a huge creative spark only to have someone interrupt you and ruin your momentum. It's never the same when you get back into it."

Raphael dropped his pen on his work and turned his chair so that his body faced Gabriel. "What is it that I can do for you, Gabe?"

Gabriel stepped into the office. He looked around, at the desks, at the walls, at the ceiling. He spoke. "Raphael ... what do you do here?" Looking down at Raphael, Gabriel could see a look of concern. He quickly added, "Don't worry, I'm not saying that you're not doing enough or anything like that — I'm genuinely curious as to what you do, what you're working on."

Raphael was truly perplexed. "Why do you want to know what I do, Gabe?"

Gabriel looked to the far wall and stared for a moment. Returning his gaze to Raphael, he said, "Because I don't know."

Raphael smiled and leaned back in his chair. He chuckled a bit, responding, "You know what I do."

"No," Gabriel said right away, a look of horror on his face. He paused for a moment, and then went on very slowly with exasperation in his voice. "Raphael, I legitimately do not know what you do. Please ... tell me."

The smile dropped off Raphael's face. They both remained where they were without speaking.

Gabriel quietly added, "Please."

Raphael had never seen Gabriel act like this before. Completely unsure of the situation and unsure of himself, he looked down at the floor. Looking back to Gabriel, he raised his hands slightly and dropped them back to his thighs, making a quiet slapping sound as he did so. He finally answered Gabriel. "I'm ... working on landscapes."

He hesitated for a moment. Gabriel looked on intently, so Raphael felt he should say a bit more. "Western Canada, part of North America, is my focus, and that's basically it."

Gabriel walked over and grabbed the chair from Lucifer's desk. Bringing it beside Raphael, he asked, "May I see what you're working on?" He sat down right next to Raphael.

"Sure," Raphael said, passing over some of his notes. As Gabriel flipped through the work, Raphael added, "Of course, that's a new program I'm working on, so most of that won't have any meaning to you."

Gabriel continued looking at the notes.

Raphael went on, "If you want to see some of my drawings, you may appreciate them more. I do assure you, however, that the program is a good thing."

Gabriel put the notes down. "I believe you, Raphael," he said, a hint of frustration in his voice.

Raphael stared at him, Gabriel not taking his eyes off the notes. "Gabe ... what's going on? Why are you here?" he asked gently.

Gabriel looked up at the ceiling. "Raphael, I thought I was doing good." He looked Raphael in the eye. "I would come down here from time to time to see how things were going. I'd find out if anyone needed anything. I gave everyone room to grow, to expand creatively. Where did I go wrong? I mean, I don't even *know* what you're *doing*, and you can't even explain it to me."

There seemed to be no end to Raphael's confusion. He said, "But, did you go wrong? I appreciated having my creative space."

Gabriel looked down to the floor, then back up at Raphael, "Maybe you're right. Maybe it isn't my fault."

They both nodded in silence, both looking extremely worried for completely different reasons. Gabriel stood up, saying, "Anyway, I was hoping to speak to Lucifer while I was down here, but I see he's missing in action. If you see him, can you get him to call me?"

"Of course, Gabe."

Gabriel remained there momentarily, thinking. He then quietly said, "Thank you."

With that, he left the room. Raphael sat there, staring at the door for some time, trying to make some sense of what he'd just experienced. He turned back to his desk and merely stared at his notes. He suddenly realized that the only thing he now understood out of everything that Gabriel told him was about losing his creative momentum.

The more he considered it, the less he felt he should dwell on it. He really didn't have any time to spare and couldn't let anything hold him back, as bizarre as the exchange was. He slowly collected his thoughts and reorganized his desk. Content with the way everything looked, he got back to work.

After working for not even five minutes, his train of thought was once again interrupted, this time by someone's angry voice coming from the doorway. "Are you Lucifer?"

Raphael closed his eyes, groaned under his breath, and dropped his pen. Opening his eyes, he turned to face the angel in the entrance, saying, "No, I'm not Lucifer."

"Do you know who I am?" the angel asked, a stern look on his face.

Raphael looked him up and down. "No. I'm sorry, but I don't believe we've met."

"My name's Michael."

Raphael smiled. "Oh, the manager of the Marketing department? How's it going? I'm Raphael."

Raphael held out his hand, but Michael did not reach out, not even pretending to want to exchange pleasantries.

Michael said, "Great, but have you seen Lucifer? Did he say where he'd be?"

Raphael thought about it. "To be honest," he answered, "I haven't really seen him all week. I don't think he's even been in the office for about two days, at least not while I've been in here."

"Anyway, here's my card." Michael handed it to Raphael. "If he comes in, get him to call me. And tell him he'd better have an amazing explanation."

Michael started to leave, but Raphael stopped him. "Wait a second, what's that supposed to mean? What has he done?"

Michael turned his head back to face Raphael, stopping, but keeping his body aimed at the door, still wanting to leave the room at the first possible opportunity. He sighed. "I think that a more appropriate question that you should be asking is 'What *hasn't* he done?'"

Raphael leaned back in disbelief. "Who, Lucifer? There's got to be a mistake."

"You know what?" Michael replied, now turning his body fully around. "That's *exactly* what Gabriel said the first time I brought this up. I thought that was just a problem with him, but you're showing me that it's a much deeper-seated problem within the department."

He paused briefly, stepping closer to Raphael before he went on. "No one listens ... when there's a legitimate concern with one of the employees."

"Well, it's not that we aren't listening," Raphael clarified the point for Michael. "It's just that ... if you knew Lucifer as well as I do, you would understand." Raphael thought about it briefly then continued, "Everything you're telling me sounds completely ludicrous."

Michael's eyes widened. "Ludicrous?" he said. Much louder this time, he repeated, "Ludicrous? I'll tell you what's *ludicrous*. The fact that this angel is doing what he's doing and no one seems to care..." He finished his thought much more softly, "That's ludicrous."

He pulled out a notepad and shook it for Raphael to see, "You know what I have here? *Seventeen* complaints filed against – oh, let's take a look." Opening it up, he started flipping through each page as he spoke, "Lucifer from R&D ... Lucifer from R&D ... Lucifer from R&D."

He stopped what he was saying to carefully look over the next entry. He began to read it verbatim. "'The angel from R&D, I don't remember his name, but I think it was Lucifer or something like that.' No, the fact that we can all turn a blind eye ... so close to our launch ... and just expect everything to work out..."

Michael put away his notepad, continuing, "*That* is what I'd call ludicrous."

They stared at each other, not adding anything to the conversation. Raphael felt the weight of Michael's words; it still seemed foreign to him that Lucifer would be the cause of so many problems, but he began to realize that, somehow, in some way, the things that Michael was telling him were real.

"Have you checked to see if he had any meetings booked today?" Raphael eventually asked.

"Of course I did, and, yes, he did have a few booked," Michael answered. Continuing with heavy sarcasm, "But wouldn't you know it? The Amazing Lucifer, in whom the Research department has so much faith, felt it unnecessary to show up to a single one."

More silence followed the remark.

"So please, Raphael, get him to give me a call," Michael finished his thought.

Raphael nodded. Seeing that all was now understood, Michael turned around and walked away.

Chapter 11

The Learning Process

Where Gabriel's visit had ruined Raphael's creative momentum, the visit from Michael had stopped him dead in his tracks. Initially, Raphael attempted to get back into the swing of things, but he just couldn't. He would pick up his notes and try to get an understanding of his previous train of thought, but he just found himself worrying about Lucifer – thoughts of a Lucifer that was unknown to him singlehandedly bringing the project down from the inside kept flooding to mind. And, for some reason, concern about everything he had ever worked toward crashing down before his very eyes seemed to have a way of preventing the further progress of his current project.

There he sat for the better part of an hour, staring into space, focusing on nothing, before Lucifer finally made an appearance, bursting into the office. He slammed his briefcase down on his desk, instantly getting Raphael's attention. Raphael could honestly not believe his eyes when he turned to look. Papers were flying around the office; Lucifer clutched several loose sheets, and his briefcase closed on other pages, hanging out of the sides. The papers themselves flapped in the breeze Lucifer was creating with his vigorous movements, quickly heading behind his desk, jerking to a stop, then quickly turning just to jerk to a stop once more. He carried himself with a nervous ferocity, the likes of which Raphael had never seen before.

Lucifer, who generally took great pride in his appearance, now stood before him with unkempt hair, unshaven, wearing clothes that looked as though they had not been changed for at least three days. His untucked shirt sported a large, greasy stain over the left nipple, part of which was visible through the now-translucent area. Lucifer's pallor was much more pronounced than usual, and the bags under his eyes had grown beyond Raphael's wildest dreams. Grooming was obviously not a priority to him at this time, but what about his health? Had he not eaten for days? Not slept? To say he was a mess was definitely encroaching on the understatement of the century.

Lucifer pushed his chair aside and started opening drawers, rummaging through and closing one drawer, then moving on to another. He stopped for a moment to look up and see a dumbfounded Raphael watching his every move. Lucifer quickly said, "Don't mind me. I'm just grabbing something, and I'm on my way back out."

Raphael shook his head. "What's going on, Lucifer?"

"I don't know what you mean," Lucifer immediately replied, looking down and continuing his search.

"I've hardly seen you all week, and now Gabriel and Michael both came down here in a flap looking for you. They want you to call them."

Lucifer laughed nervously. "Yeah, okay. That's not going to happen. I have so much to do and so little time."

Raphael leaned forward, not taking his eyes off Lucifer. He continued, "I don't know what you've been up to, but this is serious, Lucifer. Angels are worried ... *I'm* worried."

Lucifer picked up his briefcase and slammed it down on the desk. Raphael jumped and started trembling ever so slightly, his heart racing. Lucifer leaned on the briefcase, bringing all his weight down on the palms of his hands, looking down as he spoke, "Look, Raphael. Things just haven't been going well." He let out a heavy sigh before continuing, "I'm — I'm trying to get everything sorted out before we launch, but everyone is standing in my way."

Raphael dared not say anything.

Lucifer looked up at him and went on. "You see, I spent the majority of the week talking to other angels working on personality, and I might as well have been talking to brick walls. I honestly thought they would have been more ... receptive ... ever since I got Charles to understand my vision, but no. No, they're all too scared. With the release date so close, no one wants to change what they're doing; they don't even *listen* to me when I tell them about it. And then there are the ones who don't understand a word that I'm saying, which are all the rest. It's ... it's ... like God made them lack basic *reason* ... basic *comprehension* ... just to get in my way."

Lucifer let his legs give out and he fell into his chair, his head leaning on the back of it and his arms flopped over the arm rests. He sighed once more, staring at the ceiling as he spoke, "And then there are the other departments."

Lucifer had always liked walking through the Manufacturing department, but that really went without saying; the vast majority of the angels in the office enjoyed the department.

Seeing the painstakingly researched projects come to life was the height of satisfaction for all those involved. And it was easy to forget the enormous scale of the whole undertaking until, say, walking through a gigantic machine shop filled wall-to-wall with copious amounts of animals, as Lucifer had done earlier in the week.

And what a spectacle that had been. The research was nearing its end, just twelve days until launch, and Manufacturing angels had been finalizing the production process. As such, the shop had been buzzing with the end products of that process, namely, all the animals in this particular room. Not only were there cats and dogs, pigs and horses, lions and elephants, bats and birds, and everything in between, but also angels upon angels running all over the place. They had been repairing malfunctioning animals and attempting to keep some semblance of order in the shop, but that was quite the task in its own right. If the animals weren't busy breeding — further testing the production process while doing so — they had been trying to devour each other.

Lucifer had chuckled as he'd watched an angel trying to keep a pack of wolves contained in one cubicle and out of the sheep cubicle beside them. At the same time, the distracted angel hadn't noticed a mountain lion slowly stalking its way into the herd of sheep. One of the wolves had perked up its head and let out a whimper as it saw the large cat grab a sheep. *Why does this cat get a free meal but the wolves get sequestered to their cubicle? Why the prejudice against wolves?* Fortunately, with the loud "baa" let out by the sheep upon being snatched up by the mountain lion, another angel had taken notice of the unfair situation and sought to correct the prejudice, firmly instructing the animal to "drop it." Surprisingly, the cat had not taken heed, growling viciously, clearly intending to hang on to its prize.

As much as he'd wanted to see this spectacle play itself out, Lucifer had had somewhere to be. He had continued his walk, passing by an angry rhinoceros knocking over desks and sending several angels flying through the air as they'd tried to subdue the savage beast. One angel had happily shouted, "I got him!" as he'd tightened a rope that he'd managed to snag around its neck. The rhino, quite unimpressed at this prospect, had decided to thrash back and forth, flipping the angel off his feet. The angel's back had slammed firmly into the wall beside them, and he'd slumped down to the ground like a sack of potatoes. Lucifer had shaken his head, entering the long hallway connecting this shop to the next one.

He'd turned a corner, continuing to walk, the sounds of chaos diminishing more and more as he got closer to the door at the end of the hall. He'd turned the doorknob and entered, and this room was a drastic change from the previous shop. Lucifer's eyes had widened at the awe-inspiring sights before him. To say the room was gigantic was a huge understatement; the only lights illuminating the room were, at first glance, small specks scattered almost randomly throughout the room, on the ceiling, walls, and even the floor. However, upon closer inspection, the lights looked like they were actually miles and miles away, if not further. Walking away from the light coming from the open door, he'd looked down. While he could still feel the floor below his feet, it had looked as if he was walking on nothing, just seeing the distant lights far below.

As he'd slowly continued his journey, he'd realized that someone was speaking. Squinting his eyes, he had seen a small group of angels some distance away from him. With the silence of the universe filling the room, he had still made out what was being said, despite the distance.

"Observe the large sphere, representing a planet. Notice how the model appears to stick to the bottom."

Realizing he was now approaching something, Lucifer had looked ahead. He had jumped when he'd focused on the large object he'd nearly walked into. A gigantic sphere, perfectly round with absolutely no markings upon it, had stood before him. Stopping, he'd merely stared at it, listening to the angel once more.

"It is not actually attached to the bottom. See? I can freely pull it away without any difficulty."

Lucifer regained his senses when he'd realized once again that he had a destination. He'd started the trek around the planet, the voice still the only sound in the room.

"Now observe as I let go; it falls, not down, as we see it, but back toward the planet.

"You see, the Gravity program is a system of attractive forces among all objects. However, the program is quite weak for small objects; it is not until you approach large ones, such as our planet here, that the effects become pronounced and things will fall toward them. As such, there is no true 'up' or 'down' in the universe we are creating; everything is merely a frame of reference.

"Now let me direct your attention to the general layout of the universe. Even larger objects, such as the planets, will be affected in such a way if other, sufficiently large objects are close enough to exert the force upon them. The sun being the largest—"

The loud thud of Lucifer walking into the wall had been heard by them all, interrupting the speaker's train of thought. Lucifer had rubbed his nose and looked ahead; he had missed the wall at first glance, with the lights appearing to go on a great distance beyond the barrier. However, he had then seen the door several feet away, appearing out in the open, appearing to lead nowhere. As he'd made his way over to the exit, he'd heard the angel continue.

"The sun being largest, it will exert the greatest amount of force, but the other planets, their respective moons, and other large objects in the solar system will be expertly placed to keep the system in balance."

Lucifer had closed the door. The shop in which he'd then stood caused him the greatest amount of excitement that he'd felt in a long while. The large room was almost entirely filled wall to wall with humans. Lucifer had smiled. None of the humans had moved; none of them had breathed. They lacked the spark of life that would define them. Lucifer had felt goose bumps run up his arms. They were empty shells ripe for his shaping.

He had wandered slowly along the cusp of the field of humans, briefly staring into each lifeless eye along the way. They were all beautiful, perfect. Missing an arm.

Missing an arm? Lucifer had had to double check. The quick glance had not lied: One of the humans had lacked his left arm. Rather than being attached to the human, the arm had lain on a workbench in pieces, an angel diligently working away at it. She had pulled it apart, studying it carefully, ensuring everything was where it should be — muscles, arteries, nerves — and making adjustments the whole while. Not bothering her, Lucifer had continued his journey, along with his admiration of that which stood before him.

Lucifer had stepped through the open door of an office. An angel sat at the desk inside, squinting through his bifocals at the pile of papers and blueprints upon it. The angel hadn't looked up, concentrating hard with a hand upon his forehead as he'd leaned forward. Lucifer had knocked on the door.

The angel had looked up, bearing a disgruntled expression. The look was short-lived, however; recognizing the intruder, his face had relaxed and changed to a smile. "Lucifer," he'd said.

"Hey, Isaac," Lucifer had responded.

"What brings you to my neck of the woods?" Isaac from Manufacturing had asked, removing his glasses and placing them down on the pile of papers. "Please tell me you come bearing some finished personality programs."

Lucifer had laughed. "I wish. I actually came—"

"Because, let me tell you," Isaac had interrupted, shifting his weight in his chair and pointing at Lucifer as he did so. "Most of the engineers, including yours truly, are getting a bit antsy here. Launch isn't really that far off, Lucifer. We have only twelve days to finish this."

"Have you seen that animal shop, Isaac?" Lucifer had asked, pointing behind him. "It would probably be just as crazy in your shop should all those humans be conscious."

"Lucifer, we're not talking about mindless animals here. I think we will be able to maintain some sense of order with the humans."

Lucifer had not responded; he'd just nodded in silence. Eventually, he'd said, "Anyway, I'll have the program done before launch, I promise you. I'm just ... ironing out a few things."

Isaac from Manufacturing had nodded. Lucifer had added, "And everything will be functional and compatible with the physiology we designed. Don't worry."

Isaac had smiled. "I trust you, Lucifer. It's just, you know ... exciting. I can't wait until we're done."

Lucifer had returned the smile, saying, "Anyway, why I'm here: I need a favor from you, Isaac."

Isaac had leaned back in his chair, "Sure, Lucifer. Shoot."

Lucifer had hesitated, considering the best way to tell him. "I need you to ... make humans fragile," he'd said.

Isaac's eyebrows had gone down. "I don't exactly know what you mean."

Lucifer had sighed, "You know, make them fragile ... make them vulnerable. It needs to be easy for a human to lose his life. Humans should be unsafe, unprotected ... so that they are often put in uncomfortable situations in which they may very well ... die."

Isaac hadn't moved an inch while he'd taken this all in. After a moment of silent thought, a huge smile had found its way back to his face and he'd laughed and laughed. A tear coming to his eye, he'd chuckled as he spoke. "That's a good one, Lucifer. No, really, what is it I can help you with?"

No change in expression from Lucifer, he'd answered, "I'm serious, Isaac."

Isaac had stopped his laughter. He'd raised up his arms slightly, with his palms out to Lucifer. "Come on, Lucifer. What's this really about?"

"Exactly what I told you," Lucifer had replied.

Bringing his arms back down to his armrests, Isaac had raised his eyebrows, asking, "Seriously?"

Lucifer had nodded, simply saying, "Yes."

Isaac had finally understood. "Why would you want me to do that, Lucifer?" he'd responded.

Lucifer had nodded silently as he'd considered the best way to tell Isaac. He'd eventually said, "Because it needs to be done."

With Isaac looking skeptical, Lucifer had gone on, "Humans can't be indestructible machines, as so many angels want them to be. They must be vulnerable, as that will be an integral part of their beings."

Isaac had said, "But I can't do that."

Lucifer had ignored the statement, continuing in a louder voice, "A man will fear his mortality, but he will learn to live with it, to adapt to it. A man will know that he can easily be killed at a moment's notice, that he may go to sleep and never again awaken, and he may be paralyzed by this knowledge, by this fear. But not allowing this to take over his life will strengthen him. Learning to get past this fear will separate the strong from the weak."

Isaac had raised his voice slightly as well. "But, Lucifer, I can't do that."

Ignoring Isaac again, Lucifer had grown even louder. "Perhaps more important, this mortality will give humans a sense of inevitability. They will know that they have only a limited time on the Earth, and this will cause some – not all – to really do something while they can. Some will make the most of their limited time there."

"Lucifer!" Isaac had shouted.

Lucifer had stopped talking. Seeing he'd grabbed Lucifer's attention, Isaac had continued more softly, "I can't do that."

Annoyance had appeared on Lucifer's face. He'd shrugged, "Why not?"

Isaac had let out a long sigh. "I have orders ... We're actually doing the opposite."

"I know," Lucifer had responded, "but I want you to change things."

Isaac had laughed a bit, shaking his head. "Lucifer ... most departments have very loose directions to go on, but we don't. We are designing humans to survive." He had leaned forward, continuing, "Look at their immune systems – we're protecting humans from threats they can't even see. They're being given organs that expel wastes and toxins very efficiently. Heck, even look at the exceptional regenerative capabilities of all human tissue; even if organs are damaged beyond the point of proper regeneration, they still function on a very low percentage of operating tissue." Isaac had shaken his head. "You sound adamant about this, Lucifer, but the fact is, we can't have humans dying left and right."

They'd stood and stared at each other in silence. Lucifer then understood; he'd nodded slightly, then turned and started to walk out the door.

"Lucifer," Isaac had said, as Lucifer walked away, "I'm sorry ... I wish I could help you, but, hey, I'll see you tomorrow. I can't wait to see your progress at the meeting."

Continuing to walk away, Lucifer had turned his head. “Yeah, Isaac. Yeah, I can’t wait to do a presentation and unveil everything.” He’d stopped and turned right around. Leaning back into the office, Lucifer had added, “In fact, I’m so excited to be presenting to everyone that I might just head to the conference room *right now* and start prepping everything.” He had slowly backed his way out of the room. “I might as well do that. How can I contain my excitement? How in Heaven would anyone expect me to sleep tonight with all this anticipation?” Lucifer had spun around and walked away at a normal pace, chuckling, “Yeah, that’s a good one. I’ll *totally* be there; it’s not like I have anything better to do right now.”

Lucifer had made his way back across the shop, chuckling and shaking his head the whole way.

“Do you think the program is user-friendly enough?”

The question had been posed by Franklin, an angel from the Marketing department. Mark, the angel with whom Franklin often worked closely, had looked up from his notes as Franklin spoke.

“The Prayer program?” Mark had asked. “Why not? We’re being very clear with regards to its use in the Bible, so there’s really no excuse for a human not to know how to initiate the program. And they just decide to start it up, concentrate, and it’s up and running. It’s simple, straightforward, and intuitive; I don’t think it can really get much more user-friendly.”

“Okay,” Franklin had responded, “I just wanted to make sure before we move on.”

Hearing this, Mark’s eyes had lit up. He’d said, “So, you’re ready to talk about the response system?”

Franklin had nodded. With that, Mark had quickly cleared his notes from his desk, piling them off to the side. He had then opened a drawer, rummaged briefly, and brought out a thick file folder filled with papers. Removing the elastic band keeping it together, Mark had flipped it open, going through the papers and organizing himself.

Looking back at Franklin, Mark had begun, “I’d imagine that you have your own idea of an adequate response system for the humans’ questions and requests, but let me fly through mine, and we’ll see where we’re at.”

Franklin had nodded once more.

Mark had continued, “The response system I’ve designed is a pretty straightforward system of levels. Basically, say a human initiates the system, having a question to ask. He’ll be automatically directed to Level One. At this stage, he will be connected to an angel from the Marketing department, who will take in the question. The angel will have access to reference materials to help him come to a quick decision. I also think—”

“One second,” Franklin had interrupted. “What type of reference materials would we have for this?”

“Well,” Mark had answered, “we wouldn’t have very much to start. We’d get suggestions from angels, any angels who want input, and run them by the managers and, should He want to be involved, God. This way, we can have relevant information and sample answers at Level One angels’ fingertips to aid them in delivering a quick response. And, remember, that’s just to start. As we deal with more questions and requests, they would be added to the databank. Any previous response will be accessible at any time; not only will this make future responses easier, with the proper sorting and indexing, but it will also allow managers to carry out performance audits.”

“That’s a great idea,” Franklin had said. “That means that the more responses given, the easier it will be to be consistent and timely in the future. I like it.”

Mark had smiled. “Exactly. Ideally, we can compile an FAQ, greatly speeding up the whole process more often than not. But, anyway, where was I? Oh yeah, if the Level One angel can’t find the appropriate information or feels that the request would more accurately be addressed by another department, he can put the human on hold and consult with an angel from, say, R&D. I want to ensure that each department has a given number of angels who work the Prayer lines or, at least, are on call at all times. Of course, the human would not speak to another department; the best response would be arrived upon, and the original Marketing angel would filter the answer with the appropriate wording.

“However, not every request will be cut and dried; if it cannot be resolved in a timely manner, with the proper reference materials and consultation, it will be escalated up to Level Two. I’m hoping we can create a committee, or multiple committees, depending on the volume of difficult requests, with senior members from each department. The request will be sent to the committee, where members will discuss the nature of the problem and come to a consensus, within two business days, at which point the response will be delivered back to the human.

“And I am aware that there will be — hopefully not too many — requests that stump the committee. If no consensus is reached by the end of two business days, the request will be escalated further, to Level Three. This is where department managers will get involved, as well as God, should He so choose.”

“You know,” Franklin had said, “I think you’re about ready to pass this by Michael. I can’t see him disliking the idea, and you really need to get moving on this if we want it up in a week and a half, when we launch. I’ll do whatever I can to help, definitely.”

Mark had replied, “I’ll try very hard to get this up by launch, but it’s not the end of the heavens if there’s still more to be done. I mean, it won't be as important until there are more humans in the world. If we have to, we can communicate directly to start things out."

"And I think it's great that the system will improve over time," Franklin had added. "Ideally, fewer things should move up to the higher levels as we accumulate a larger database of responses."

Just then, Nathaniel had walked into the office. This wasn't really anything out of the ordinary, his office being just down the hall. In fact, he would often stop by — several times a day, even — just to talk. Neither Mark nor Franklin could understand that; the second they got to the office, they would begin working on projects nonstop, not really having any chance for a breather. Yet, there would be Nathaniel, relaxed and in their doorway. Maybe his time-management skills were unrivaled, or maybe he just needed some time to step away from his project to reflect before jumping back in. Either way, Mark and Franklin always welcomed the successful angel into their office; it not only gave them a much-needed break, but it also often allowed him to impart his wisdom upon them and gave them an opportunity to learn.

"Hey, Frank, Mark, what's the word?" Nathaniel had said.

They both had looked over to Nathaniel.

Mark had answered, "Oh, not too much. We're just working on a program. Can we help you with something?"

"Actually," Nathaniel had said, "if you two got a second, I'd like to borrow you."

"Can it wait a few minutes?" Mark had asked. "We're kind of busy right now."

Nathaniel had shaken his head. "That's the thing; it really can't."

Franklin and Mark had looked at each other. Looking back at Nathaniel in the doorway, Franklin had said, "Sure. What's going on?"

Nathaniel had ignored the question and motioned behind him. “Come on,” he’d said, “let’s walk and talk.”

Mark had quickly gathered up his papers and closed them in his file, putting it back in his drawer. Both he and Franklin had got up and followed Nathaniel, who was then walking down the hallway.

“Here’s the situation,” Nathaniel had imparted on them while they’d moved, “I’m sitting in my office, quietly working on my project, when I get this phone call. It’s kind of out of the blue. I’m not expecting any calls, but it’s Paul from the sixty-second floor.”

At this point, they’d reached the elevator. Nathaniel had stopped, hit the Down button, and then turned to his followers. He’d continued his story, “So, I’m talking to Paul, but he’s sounding kind of flustered. He says he needs me to head down to his floor because there’s a commotion. Apparently, some R&D angel’s pestering them.”

Ding! The elevator doors had opened, and they’d stepped inside. Nathaniel had pressed the button corresponding to the sixty-second floor. He’d gone on as the doors closed behind them, “Of course, I told him to just nicely get rid of him, but apparently he’s being really persistent.”

“Couldn’t they call Michael?” Franklin had asked. “Wouldn’t he be the one to go to about this?”

Nathaniel had turned to Franklin, saying, “Well, Paul says that Michael’s not available, or he can’t get a hold of him or something. So, naturally, he thought I could help. Anyway, I’m in the middle of stuff. I don’t want to just drop everything and head down there, but then he tells me the angel’s name is Lucifer.”

The eyebrows of the two listening angels had gone up when he spoke the name.

Nathaniel had smiled. “Of course, now I’m thinking, ‘Lucifer ... from R&D?’”

Ding! The doors had opened to floor sixty-two. All three of them had stood there momentarily. Mark had glanced back and forth between Franklin and Nathaniel before eagerly asking, “Do you think it’s the same one?”

Nathaniel had responded, “Well, how many Lucifers do you know?”

They had all stepped out of the elevator and begun to walk down the hall.

Nathaniel had turned his head to the side as he walked to continue the conversation with the angels following him. “And, let me tell you, once I found out it was Lucifer from R&D, I came right away; it would be my *pleasure* to eject that prick from the department. I figured it would probably be a good idea to bring a few angels along, just in case it turns ugly. I wouldn’t expect either of you to have to do much but, in my experience, he’s ... unpredictable. You never know.”

While Franklin and Mark had both winced a bit at the word “unpredictable,” they’d relished the opportunity to see Nathaniel sort the problem out. They were then beginning to understand what they were in for. Ahead had come the sound of someone shouting, growing louder and louder as they’d approached. They had turned a corner, and there Paul had stood, nervously awaiting them. Nathaniel had pointed ahead, raising his eyebrows; Paul had given him a nod, following as the three of them had passed.

Only then could the shouting become comprehensible: “...by giving them constant reminders of Him, of *us,* you’re not letting them accomplish anything with their lives!”

“I already told you there’s nothing I can do!” another voice had shouted back.

“We need to cause humans to doubt!” the first voice had yelled.

They had gone around the corner to see that it was Lucifer, the same Lucifer from R&D who Nathaniel had hoped would be there.

Lucifer had continued to shout, “They must rely on faith!”

Nathaniel had taken no time in springing into action. He had quickly approached Lucifer, shouting, “Hey! Hey!”

Lucifer had spun around to face Nathaniel. Lucifer’s brow had been furrowed, and his eyes piercing. Nathaniel had immediately felt the hatred wash all over him. Never before had he seen such a look. Nathaniel’s subconscious had begged him to just flee the scene, but being the master of self-control that he was, he’d stayed strong.

With the shouting on hold for the time being, Nathaniel had quieted his voice but remained stern, nonetheless. “I’m going to ask you once ... to calm down and take a seat in that chair.”

Lucifer had continued to stare into Nathaniel’s eyes for a moment, gazing deep into his soul, studying it thoroughly. No one had spoken, no one had moved, no one had taken a single breath. He had then looked around him, behind Nathaniel, and saw what he was up against. Then fully understanding that the battle was over, he had done exactly what had been asked of him.

Lucifer had taken his seat, and the look of unbridled rage had quickly dissolved from his face. Only then did everyone take the opportunity to breathe once more.

Nathaniel had said nothing; instead, he had slowly walked past Lucifer, grabbing a chair. He had brought it in front of the angel and taken his time to sit down. Nathaniel had then just looked at Lucifer, shaking his head. Lucifer showed no emotion.

Nathaniel had turned to the angel Lucifer had been only recently arguing with and calmly asked, “Now, what’s going on here?”

Lucifer had leaned forward a bit, saying, “All I was doing was—”

Nathaniel had quickly turned back to Lucifer, raising his voice suddenly. “I wasn’t asking you.”

He had sat there angrily staring Lucifer down. Lucifer had stopped speaking, looking back at Nathaniel with his flat expression.

Nathaniel had slowly turned back to the other angel, continuing in a much gentler tone once more. "I was talking to him."

The angel had looked to Lucifer, who gave him no acknowledgment, still regarding Nathaniel only. Looking back at Nathaniel, he had said, "He basically came in here talking about how we have to get humans to doubt our existence. Something about only the faithful being worthy of God's kingdom. I told him that, even if I wanted to help him — which I didn't, by the way — any changes to any Marketing techniques need to be cleared through a senior committee, which would have to be verified by Michael before being green-lit. Of course, that wasn't good enough for him."

"There, that wasn't so bad," Nathaniel had said with a smile as he'd turned back to face Lucifer. "Even if he wanted to help you with your idiotic idea, he can't. No need to freak out, no need to create a scene; his hands are tied, that's it." He had raised his hands slightly when finishing the thought and then brought them back down to his thighs. "No, Lucifer," Nathaniel went on, "if you want to accomplish anything with your request, you need to first consult with a senior Marketing angel..." Nathaniel had placed a hand on his own chest, adding, "...like me."

He'd left his hand there momentarily and just stared in silence, waiting for the comment to sink in. Feeling that an adequate amount of time had been given to consider what had been said, he'd continued, "But I'll save you the trouble of attempting that. Did I say your idea was idiotic?" Nathaniel had lowered his eyebrows and nodded. "I think I did. No need to elaborate on it any further or try to explain in some inane way why it's important. I'm not interested. No, Lucifer, the buck stops here. I don't even want to know what you thought your little plan would accomplish in the long run. The simple fact is, you lose. And, do you know why you lose? Because you don't have connections; you don't have friends. And you're stupid.

"Funny, this all sounds strangely familiar to me. Wasn't there a time when *I* needed help with *my* project and you just shut me down? Well, didn't it ever occur to you that you might need my help with something, that you might come crawling back to me? No? Well ... that's why you're stupid.

"Just answer me one question: If you spat in my face and turned me away with such a lack of respect—" Nathaniel had leaned closer to Lucifer to finish what he was saying "—why would I ever help you?"

They had sat and stared at each other for some time. Stone-faced, Lucifer had quietly replied, "Nathaniel, do you really think you have any control over what goes on with the project? Those friends and connections you hold so dear are meaningless; all you have is the power to run on over to Michael, begging at his feet. The real question you should be asking me at this time is 'What possible use can *you* be to *me*?'"

Lucifer had looked away from Nathaniel and stood up. He had quietly and confidently walked out of the office. A path had cleared as he went, no angel remaining in his way, no angel looking him in the eye.

Charles had sat at his desk, scribbling notes frantically; frustration could be felt emanating from every pore on his body. He was then coming to the realization that he still had a lot to do with the humans before the launch, just nine days away, and he didn't have time to be running around pleading with the other angels for Lucifer's sake.

"So how did it go?"

The question had almost made Charles jump out of his skin.

Charles had looked up to find Lucifer sitting in the chair across from him.

"Lucifer," Charles had said, "you scared me; I didn't even hear you come in."

Lucifer had merely raised his eyebrows, repeating himself slowly. "How did it go?"

"Oh, not well at all," Charles had answered. "The angels with the snowflake program were quite ... apprehensive at the request to adapt their program."

Lucifer had frowned and shaken his head.

Charles had gone on, "They wouldn't give it to me, Lucifer. In fact, *no one* gave me any help all week. I don't know, Lucifer..."

"What don't you know?"

Charles had shaken his head and brought up his hands slightly, opening his mouth as he had tried to come up with the proper words. Eventually, he had found them. "I ... maybe we're wrong."

"No, we're not," Lucifer had responded immediately, continuing to shake his head, not looking at Charles.

Charles had kept his gaze focused on Lucifer. "But how can you say that? Not one other angel agrees with us—" Charles had looked away, continuing, "—and I think I'm starting to see their point."

Lucifer's face had snapped back toward Charles. He had pointed at him while he spoke harshly. "Don't talk like that. In your heart, you know I'm right."

Charles's face had slowly drifted back toward Lucifer. Looking at him and his outstretched finger, Charles had asked, "Do I?"

Lucifer had retracted his finger and dropped his hand on his thigh. He had let out a long, slow, heavy sigh and eventually said, "Let me try talking to them, the snowflake angels. Maybe I can get them on board..." Tears had welled up in Lucifer's eyes, but he had done his best to hold them back. "Just..." He had trailed off, trying to maintain his composure. "Don't give up on me."

He had sat there momentarily, looking into Charles's eyes. Lucifer had felt his hands shaking ever so slightly on his thighs. With all his might, still staring at Charles, Lucifer had flexed the muscles in his arms and his hands until the shaking came to a stop. With that, he had slowly stood up. He had nodded slightly, muttering under his breath, "Don't give up on me."

Lucifer had turned and made his way out of the office. Fortunately for him, the snowflake angels' offices were nearby. He had wandered down the hallway to the office of James, the snowflake angel with whom Lucifer was the most familiar. Coming to the door, he'd knocked, only to find nobody sitting at the desk.

"Hello?" Lucifer had said, sticking his head into the office and looking around.

No one had been there. Lucifer had been about to turn around when he'd noticed a notebook in the middle of the desk. He had walked over to it and sat down, opening the book.

"It was the snowflake program," Lucifer said, looking at Raphael as he spoke. "So, naturally, I took it upon myself to borrow the notes, photocopying everything I needed."

Raphael was shocked, and Lucifer could clearly see that.

Lucifer added, "Don't worry; I brought the notebook back before it was missed." He sighed. "I'm starting to realize that the only way I'll ever see this thing through is by taking matters into my own hands."

Lucifer, finished his stories, merely sat there staring at Raphael. Never feeling nervous under his gaze before, something didn't sit well with Raphael at this time. Lucifer was acting very strange, and Raphael legitimately did not like it.

"What about you?" Lucifer asked. "What have you been working on all week?"

Raphael answered, slowly, "I've been working on this new program." He then quickly added, "But, I won't get into details; it won't mean much to you right now."

Still leaning back in his chair, Lucifer lazily held out his hand. "Let me see it."

Reluctantly, Raphael slid closer to Lucifer, giving him the notes. Lucifer snatched them up immediately and started flipping through very quickly. "Just at a glance, you're changing your landscapes with time," Lucifer stated, his eyes moving back and forth as he skimmed the documents.

"Yes," responded Raphael.

Lucifer dropped the notes on his desk. Seeing Raphael reach out to get them back, Lucifer shifted forward in his chair, picking them up once again and handing them off. "Just make sure you don't dwell too much on every single detail right now," he said.

Raphael lowered his eyebrows. "Why not?"

Lucifer shrugged. "Because you'll drive yourself crazy. Plus, you don't really have the time to worry about it. The way I see it ... May I see the notes again?"

Raphael handed them back to him. Lucifer started flipping through once more.

"I would just imagine that every fix you make will do something detrimental somewhere else down the line, like, even to another landscape." He pointed at something on one of the pages. "There, you see? It looks like this is the case."

Looking back up at Raphael, he continued, "It just seems to me like you have the wrong ... focus right now, if you intend to have this up and running in a week's time."

Raphael considered what Lucifer was saying. "Then what do you propose I do to fix it?"

Lucifer shrugged once more. "I guess what would make sense to me would be to alter the overall intention of the program. It seems like the only viable way to get it going in time to launch would be to make less of a program you can just set up and leave doing its thing and more of one to make landscape maintenance much easier."

What Lucifer was telling him was starting to sink in.

Lucifer added, "Maybe do some tests focusing not just on the end result of each change you make but, rather, the general effect each tweak has on several test landscapes. Note any trends you find, and then shift your focus on making the program more user-friendly, affecting different regions independently. That way, each angel can sort of have it running with background settings that suit their respective landscapes, and they can tweak it as they see fit, even turning it off should they so choose."

Raphael was astonished. He had no idea what he could possibly say or do following what Lucifer had just imparted upon him. Lucifer got up and walked around the desk, giving Raphael his papers. He then turned around and grabbed his things.

Looking at Raphael once more, Lucifer said, "Anyway, I have a lot to do. I'll see you some other time."

With that, he walked away.

Chapter 12

Holding On

"Lucifer, you're a wreck."

Lucifer snapped his eyes open, heavy as they were. He sat at the counter in the Pearly Gates, perched atop his barstool, leaning forward, the entire weight of his head resting in his open palm. Blinking repeatedly in short succession, he eventually managed to focus his eyes on the figure of Peter standing in front of him. Lucifer sat up straight and rubbed his face vigorously up and down with both hands simultaneously. Only then did he take the opportunity to say something.

"No, I'm just tired ... and overworked. Take a good look at me in five days' time, and I'll be the picture of good health."

He hesitated and thought about what he had said. He went on. "Maybe seven days; I'll probably need to sleep nonstop for two full days after a week like I'm anticipating."

Peter pushed several of Lucifer's loose papers out of his way and leaned forward on the counter. He sighed. "If you say so, Lucifer."

"What do you mean by that?"

Peter looked down at the mess of papers piled all over his bar, then back up at Lucifer. Licking his lips and smacking them together once before going on, he said, "Do you ... deep down ... really think that everything is going to go back to the way it was, after all this?" Peter took a step back and waved his hands all around, motioning to the notes upon notes, and motioning to Lucifer himself.

Lucifer's eyes widened, and Peter could see that he knew exactly what he was talking about. But Lucifer immediately composed his face again, closing off his feelings, controlling his emotions.

"Peter, you are completely right," he answered. "Deep down, I *know* things can never go back." He paused. After blinking several times, Lucifer continued more softly, "Deep down, I know that I'm not the same angel I was a month ago ... but, I guess I like having a bit of denial in my life. It really feels good to think that I can go back to those simpler times. Can you let me have that?"

Peter let out a heavy sigh. He stared into Lucifer's eyes for some time, and they both continued their conversation merely through their gazes. Conceding, Peter eventually nodded slowly and then walked away.

Peter had sparked something in Lucifer; he had not truly considered it until that point. Denial. He had taken great comfort in denial before, but that time was over. He now realized that he had to shed the security of denial if he was to move forward, to make the most of this time to grow.

I am changing, Lucifer thought. *I am evolving. To be in denial, to go back, would be a step in the wrong direction. To live in denial would be to limit my potential, to limit every single thing I am capable of. Think of what I can do with a life,* my *life, free of denial. No, living in denial, I would be no better than...*

His eyes widened once again with this realization. He turned his gaze to the rows and rows of bottles making up the shelves beyond the bar. He allowed his sight to become unfocused; he allowed the world to become blurry, and he watched as the different colors and shapes blended together, all becoming one. *I would be no better than* ... His thoughts trailed off once more.

I understand.

At this time, Mary wandered into the bar. Seeing Lucifer sitting there, she came over to him. She pulled out the stool beside him and gently touched his arm, saying, "Lucifer?"

He turned to her, his vision still out of focus. He sat for a moment, staring at the blur of the angel beside him, and spoke quietly. "I understand."

Her hand still on his arm, she replied, "What do you understand, Lucifer?"

He came back to reality and focused his vision, only now seeing that the jumbled shape in front of him was actually Mary. "Mary!" a surprised Lucifer stated, ignoring her question. "What are you doing here?"

"I've been looking all over for you," she answered. "I couldn't find you anywhere, but I got ahold of Raphael, and he mentioned something about the Pearly Gates, so here I am." She looked him up and down before going on. "Lucifer, I'm worried about you."

He looked away from her, back to the bottles behind the bar. He shook his head, quickly speaking. "No, you don't have to worry. I'm fine; I've never been better."

"No, Lucifer," Mary replied. "I don't know how you can say that. Have you looked at yourself in the mirror?"

She pointed at the mirror at the back of the bar, behind the bottles. He decided to humor her and looked at himself, moving his head up and down, side to side, appearing to carefully study the reflection. Having taken what he considered to be an adequate amount of time, he turned back to her.

Mary continued, "You're getting too involved in the project. You stopped caring about your friends. You stopped caring about your *life*."

She could see that he didn't care about a single word that came out of her mouth. It didn't matter; this was important. She went on. "You stopped caring about *us*."

He raised his eyebrows. "Is *that* what this is about? You can't comprehend what I'm accomplishing here. Of course I care more about the project than anything else. The project is big; it's bigger than *me* ... it's bigger than *you*."

He raised his hands to help her visualize what he was talking about. "It's bigger than anything you can imagine." He paused, staring in her face to ensure that she was listening before continuing. "So, maybe I stopped caring about everything else ... but nothing else matters."

She sighed. "You need to stop. You can't handle ... whatever it is that God's having you do."

"Why do you care?"

His tone suddenly made her feel that he despised her. Mary looked away from him and shrugged. Turning back, she said, "I guess I don't want to see you ruining your life."

"Don't you realize, Mary? I'm not ruining my life ... I'm not ruining anything." Lucifer leaned in to tell this to her. "I'm *improving* ... I'm *evolving*."

"How can you believe that?" she shouted. She put a hand to her mouth, trying to compose herself. Looking away, she quietly added, "Don't you want to go back to the way things were?"

He shook his head. "No, Mary. And even if I did, we're long past the point of no return. Even ask Peter; he knows."

Mary shook her head. "But, Lucifer, we're never too far along to fix things. You're saying you can't go back only because you *believe* it's true." She looked away. "I'm fighting for you, Lucifer. Can't you see that? I'm fighting to try to save you. I'm not doing this for me ... I'm doing this for *you*."

She returned her gaze to Lucifer. Leaning closer to him, she continued speaking. "Think about everyone you know ... think of how Raphael feels ... think about *us*."

He looked across the bar and abruptly said, "There is no 'us.'"

Mary froze. The strength of his words hit her across the face like a sledgehammer. For the first time in this conversation, Mary knew that he was right. It was over. She had nothing left to say, nothing left to do. Remaining at his side only momentarily, she looked away from him. She stood up, her face like granite. Not turning toward him, not looking back, she started slowly walking away and simply said, "Goodbye, Lucifer."

He turned to face her and witnessed her gradually disappearing form. "Goodbye?" he said. He repeated much louder, "Goodbye?"

Lucifer chuckled a bit to himself. He shouted across the bar at her. "Don't say goodbye; this isn't a goodbye. Why, I'll be seeing you soon ... *very* soon. I'm sure I'll be up at God's office tomorrow, and you'll be there. I *know* you will."

As Mary turned the corner and walked out of the Pearly Gates, she couldn't pinpoint the true cause of the great sadness she was experiencing. It may have been due to the conversation she had just had, but there was a distinct possibility that it stemmed from the fact that Lucifer had no idea what had just happened.

Chapter 13

Understanding

Ding! The elevator doors on the ninety-sixth floor opened. Mary looked up to see what she had been dreading all day: Lucifer stepped out. There was something sinister about him that gave her chills down her spine as he walked up to her desk. She closed her eyes and took a deep breath as he approached.

Lucifer didn't even acknowledge Mary as he walked with an almost zombie-like focus. He went past her desk and right up to the door to God's office, which was closed. He stood there and stared at the door, puzzled.

"*This* door is closed?" he questioned the situation. After mulling it over in his mind, he spoke to Mary directly without bothering to look at her. "This door is never closed."

She looked to the door, then to Lucifer, cautiously saying, "Yes. He told me He wasn't to be—"

Lucifer cut her off by kicking the door at the handle with all his might, the wood around the handle cracking. He gave it another sharp kick in the same place, and the wood could not hold any longer; the cracking became so severe that the area around the handle bent and the door flew open with a spray of splinters. Mary's jaw dropped, and she sprang to her feet immediately. Lucifer stayed exactly where he stood, smiling as he breathed in the glorious destruction he had brought down upon the barrier to his impending triumph.

"Don't get up, Mary," God said calmly, sitting at His desk with His hands clasped together, appearing deep in thought. "I was expecting Lucifer."

Mary looked to God, then back at Lucifer. Although she truly did not believe that would be for the best, she eventually listened and reluctantly sat down.

God asked, "Lucifer, what was it you wanted to say?"

Lucifer stepped into the office, speaking as he did so, "Oh, I think You know what I want to tell You. In fact, I *know* You know what it is that I want to say." He paused, looking back at the broken door and the mess he had caused in God's normally impeccable office. "You never close Your door. You *knew* I would kick it in, didn't You? In fact, You *wanted* me to kick it in, and apparently I didn't disappoint."

God motioned to a chair, telling Lucifer, "Have a seat."

Lucifer regarded the Lord with a look of horror. "No," he said, stopping to continue looking upon the Lord with his face frozen in place, to fully display the sense of repugnance he was feeling at the order before continuing, "No, I don't want to sit down. I'm fine standing."

He thought about what was happening and went on. "And You knew that. You *knew* I'd refuse, but You offered me a seat anyway." Lucifer shook his head. "You see, the problem here is that I'm starting to understand."

"And that's why you're here, isn't it?"

Lucifer shook his head once more in disbelief, growing impatient. "Why would You ask me that? You know why I'm here."

God looked as though He was pondering the situation, Lucifer's impatience growing as he waited for the Lord to say something. Eventually, He spoke. "Why don't you talk about it, Lucifer? It will make you feel better."

"Are You sure about that?" Lucifer asked sarcastically.

God merely nodded.

"Why don't You start me off?" Lucifer continued. "You seem to be much more able to properly express Yourself than *I* am."

"Okay, if that's what you want," God said. "You're scared, Lucifer."

"Of course I'm scared! That was an inevitability! I'm so flooded with emotions right now that fear was bound to be a part of it. But, why focus on the fear?"

"Because fear is the most pronounced at this time. I can feel it, Lucifer."

Lucifer stepped closer, a mischievous smile growing on his face. He pointed at God as he spoke. "But now I understand." He stopped to emphasize the point, even though he was well aware of whom he was talking to. Lucifer continued, "I understand ... what it is ... to be You."

They remained where they were, Lucifer now balancing all his weight on the back of the chair that was offered to him with his finger aimed squarely at the Lord. "You said You knew what it was to be me," Lucifer added, "and I truly did not understand how that was possible at the time ... but now I get it. You felt what I felt every step of the way, but it's more than that. You are experiencing what I experienced at every single stage of my life ... at this very second..." The smile still on his face, Lucifer shook his head before finishing the thought, "...along with everything else."

He grew calmer. "You know, You were right; I should have had more faith in You, more faith in the project. I just didn't understand, but who can blame me? It's a lot for one angel to wrap his feeble mind around. However, I am beyond that now;

I get it. You know that the project will turn out ... 'to Your liking' ... because You can see it. You're looking at it right now, aren't You? You're experiencing everything, taking it all in."

Lucifer began to walk beside God's desk slowly, not looking at Him, still speaking. "But *You* ... You don't truly understand. I know that now. You experience everything we all do, but never on its own, never in a vacuum. You experience life through a filter, living vicariously through the other angels..."

He turned and faced God, shouting, "Through *me!*"

Lucifer kept staring at Him, looking at Him with a combination of contempt and disgust. He turned away and continued his walk, past God's desk and past God into realms unknown. God merely sat and listened, not following Lucifer as he moved.

Lucifer mused on. "Sure, I feel the same emotions I used to feel but, with this ... flood ... of emotions ... I don't experience them in the same way.

"I understand. You aren't anything like us angels, and You want to understand us. But, God, I hate to tell You: You're losing touch with the angels."

Lucifer reached the large window. For the first time in his life, he decided that he would peer out, to see the glorious view as God would, to become a god, even for a moment. He leaned forward, pressing up against the window, well aware that he was leaving greasy handprints, but all the while not caring. Lucifer was amazed by the view; he could really see all of Heaven vividly from up there. The angels were so minuscule, mirroring the way he now regarded them on a day-to-day basis.

He regained his train of thought. "You want to pretend You are like us. So You do these superficial things, like having this conversation with me, all of which You either never required or have long evolved beyond the point of needing. And why? So that You don't lose touch."

Lucifer turned around, facing God's chair. He stared at the back of it, his mind peering right through, seeing a motionless God on the other side. He began walking back, going on as he did so, "But, You need to realize that this pretending is hurting Yourself; living in denial is limiting Your true potential, and I can finally see that."

Reaching God's desk, Lucifer knocked on it loudly. "Do You need this desk?" He brought his hands up, looking back and forth and motioning all around him, saying, "This office?"

God watched him but gave no indication of feeling any emotion.

Running his fingers along God's sleeve, Lucifer continued his questioning. "Do You need these clothes?" Lucifer peered into God's eyes with a look of displeasure. "Do You need this body?"

Receiving no response to any of his questions, he answered them himself. "No, You don't need any of these things. You *limit* Yourself."

Lucifer hopped up on God's desk, sitting finally. He laughed. "Really, how can so many regard a being as perfect when He limits Himself in so many ways?" He turned his gaze away from the Lord and focused on the small painting upon His wall. He sighed. "I'm beginning to lose touch. With the torrent of emotions I'm feeling, with my newfound sense of understanding, I'm losing a sense of my ... angelic self. Of course I'm scared. I don't think I've ever been so frightened in my entire life, now that I'm beginning to observe everything in a different light ... as *You* would."

He came down from the desk, more excitement in his voice. "I'm not like them anymore."

"You never were." God finally spoke, His face still emotionless.

Lucifer continued, ignoring God's comment. "But, frightening as it is, I can't dwell on it. I'm changing. I'm *evolving*. And keeping that out of mind would be to limit myself — to limit my *potential*. But I won't. I will continue to sprout, to grow, to flourish until *I* grow beyond the need for clothes ... beyond the need of a body, and beyond."

Lucifer approached God. Kneeling beside Him, he said, with a whisper, "I will continue to evolve until I understand *everything*."

He moved in closer, still speaking with a whisper, "But now I know ... I *understand*."

Putting his lips so close to God's ear that he touched it as he spoke, he said, "You feel pain ... You feel hatred..."

He quickly went behind God's chair and came around to His opposite ear, placing his hand firmly on God's shoulder, softly saying, "You feel fear ... and You're feeling it right now."

Lucifer moved his hands to God's armrest and leaned back slightly. He went back to a normal speaking voice. "How can one who is so powerful — a perfect being, in fact — feel fear?"

He looked at God quizzically, awaiting a response, but God gave him no satisfaction.

Lucifer went on. "What would the angels think if they knew You, the Creator — their perfect leader — felt fear?"

He lowered his voice to mimic that of another generic angel, "'Impossible.'"

Returning to his normal voice, he continued, "They'd say — but, you know what would happen? Some would consider it, and they would question it, and they would start to question everything they ever believed in.

"And then the few would be standing before You as I am today. I'll bet You can see them right now. Are You looking at them? What are they saying? Do their thoughts mirror my own?"

He stood up, still staring at God all the while. Lucifer shook his head, confessing, "The only thing I don't understand is why."

God still sat silently, unflinching.

Lucifer yelled, "Why are You doing this to me?"

Still no answer.

Lucifer shouted, "Is it a game? Some sort of sick fantasy? Or do You have some sort of ... higher agenda for which I'm Your perfect tool?"

God said nothing.

Lucifer dropped to his knees and clutched the armrest. "Was it as simple as fixing the project, or is it some huge, convoluted plan, the scope of which I can never fathom?"

He waited for a response. Receiving no answer, he shouted, "Tell me!"

God sat there, staring into Lucifer's eyes. His lips slowly came to life and He gently said, "You know that I can't."

They both felt Lucifer's desperation; the weight of his burden pressed down hard upon each of them. Still staring into God's eyes, a single tear came to Lucifer's right eye, slowly falling down his cheek. With all the remaining strength he could muster, Lucifer said, "I know that You *won't*."

Michael stood in the hallway, impatiently awaiting the elevator. His mind was going a mile a minute thinking about all the things that had to be done to have everything and everyone ready for the impending release. He wished the elevator would stop taking its sweet time, because he was a busy angel. He had a million things to do, so he had only an extremely limited period of time to use in order to grab a quick bite to eat and to down about a gallon of coffee in order to keep things going in the afternoon.

Ding! The elevator doors opened, and Michael stepped inside, immediately pushing the button for the ground floor.

The doors closed, and the elevator slowly took the restless angel closer to his destination. Standing there for only a moment, Michael thought he heard something peculiar: the sound of someone sobbing. He turned, only now noticing that he was, in fact, not alone in the elevator. A small mound in the corner was actually another angel. The angel was curled up, his head buried deep within his arms, crying. Not sure of himself, Michael turned back to face the front of the elevator. Doing so gave Michael another peculiar revelation: No other buttons were lit up on the front panel. This angel, thoroughly defeated for whatever reason, had just come into this box, sat in the corner, and cried.

Michael grew nervous, feeling that he should say or do something to help this angel in his time of need, but he froze up. He really just wanted to run, to get out of this uncomfortable situation, but he knew deep down that he could do so much more. Heavy sobbing filled the elevator, only to be broken up by gasps for breath in order to make way for more crying. Michael looked at the panel at the front of the elevator, seeing that they were nearing the ground floor. He looked back to the broken angel and sighed a heavy sigh, deciding to act.

Michael stepped toward the panel of buttons and pressed the emergency stop. Immediately, the elevator became motionless, jerking as it did so. This seemed to surprise the other angel, who jumped as it happened. Michael stood there observing him, but the angel dared not look up.

Slowly, Michael made his way over to the angel until he stood immediately beside the crumpled mound that made up his entire being. Michael leaned against the back wall and slowly lowered himself until he was sitting next to the angel, on the floor of the elevator. Without any hesitation, Michael put his hand on the angel's back and rubbed it gently.

Michael spoke softly, "You know what? I know times are tough."

The angel still would not look at him.

Michael continued, "We all have bad days, horrible days. There have been days where I ... wasn't sure if I could carry on." Michael looked up at the ceiling of the elevator, thinking of what to say next. It came to him. "But you know what? Life goes on. If you persevere, you'll find that everything works out."

He returned his gaze to the broken angel and raised his voice to a normal speaking volume. "Life is far from perfect, I know, but you can't let life defeat you. You just have to go out there and do what you know in your heart you have to do." He looked away again, and quietly added, "And damn the consequences."

A muffled voice came out of the mess beside him. "That is so true."

The angel finally raised his head and looked upon Michael. Tears running down his face, his eyes red from crying, he wiped his face as best as he could with his sleeve before adding, "That is *so* true."

Michael smiled at the angel and patted him on the shoulder. Pride swelling in his heart because he had successfully coaxed the angel out, he said, "Everything's going to be fine."

The angel returned what appeared to be his best attempt at a smile. Michael asked him, "What's your name?"

"Lucifer," came the reply.

Michael's eyebrows lowered. He wanted to make sure he had heard the angel correctly. "Lucifer?"

The angel nodded.

Michael added, "From R&D?"

The changing tone caused Lucifer to become much more cautious in his answer. "Yes ... why?"

Michael suddenly felt unclean. He jumped back up to his feet and took a step away from Lucifer. "If you're Lucifer from

R&D," Michael said in his usual authoritative voice, "then you have a lot of explaining to do."

Lucifer suddenly picked up an air of confidence. "And just who do you think you are?"

"In case you didn't know, I'm the manager of the Marketing department. Guess what? I've received quite a number of complaints about you."

Lucifer now knew full well where this was going, but he was not prepared to be spoken to in this manner. He started propping himself up against the wall, standing up slowly, speaking as he did so. "You know, just because you're a manager and you're given that title..." Now on his feet, Lucifer looked Michael square in the eye and finished his thought. "It doesn't make you important like you think it does."

Michael found himself somewhat surprised at this; no one had ever talked to him this way.

Lucifer went on. "Guess what? You're nothing."

"You watch your tone with me," Michael responded. "If I didn't know any better, I'd say you were trying to bring the project down from the inside."

"Then I guess you're stupider than you look," Lucifer retorted. "If you knew anything, you would see that I'm saving the project from all the other angels."

Michael shook his head. "You pompous meathead. I can't believe anyone could be so blind. I'm going to spend the rest of the time up to the release seeing that no one helps you, and that no one even likes you. In fact, they'll all be so scared of you that they won't even talk to you. I will see to it personally that you can't do any damage to the humans or anything else you try to get your grubby little hands on."

Lucifer stepped closer to Michael, so close that their noses were almost touching. He said, "As the manager of the Marketing department, I think you should probably have bigger fish to fry at this time. How can you be so sure that

Marketing will be able to finish everything they need to do if you're busy worrying about little ol' me?"

Lucifer banged on the button panel with his fist. Michael didn't see what he had done, but he felt the elevator come to life again. It hardly moved before coming to a stop, and the doors opened to floor fourteen.

Lucifer put out his hand to stop them from closing and said, "Just as a warning to you — not a threat, no, but a warning — you'd better explicitly tell the humans how they should act, because when I'm finished with them, they won't be able to figure it out for themselves."

With that, he walked out. As the doors were closing, he heard Michael yell, "This isn't over! When *I'm* finished with you, you aren't even going to have a job!"

Chapter 14

Putting a Stop to It

"Stocking up on toilet paper, I see." Isaac spoke to the only angel in his line as he rang in her items. "I'm the same way, though. If you run out once, you never want to make that same mistake again."

A grin came to her face as he spoke, but she didn't reply.

After scanning the final item, he said, "And ... forty-two fifteen is your total."

She handed Isaac some bills. He punched the amount into the computer, causing the till to open, and gave the change to the angel.

With that, he said, "Now hurry on home; the forecast's calling for rain, and I don't want you to get caught in it."

Still grinning, she simply said, "Thanks."

The angel took her bags and went on her way, the bell above the door dinging as she exited. Isaac looked around and saw that it was quiet in the store this evening, much like the average evening. He wasn't a huge fan of the evening shifts, as the time went much more slowly than during the days, but someone had to work them. He made the best of them anyway; it gave him plenty of time to think.

Isaac jumped suddenly at the sound of an angel dumping his groceries on the counter. Putting his hand firmly on his chest to prevent his now rapidly beating heart from leaping out of it, he looked at the angel and smiled when he recognized the face. "Wait, don't tell me ... Lucifer? Yes, Lucifer! How are you?" Isaac excitedly said.

Lucifer simply replied, "I'm fine."

Looking him up and down quickly, Isaac wasn't completely sure of that, but he didn't dwell on it. He glanced at the items as he scanned them. "More canned goods than you usually buy. But it makes sense, I guess. Lots of busy angels lately, and I know when I don't want to cook, I tend to—"

"Please, Zack," Lucifer interrupted, "cut the crap."

Isaac really didn't know what to say. With a nervous smile, he responded, "I ... don't really know what you're talking about."

"Sure you do," Lucifer responded immediately. Seeing a confused look on Isaac's face, Lucifer added, "Oh, really? You don't know?"

Isaac shook his head.

Lucifer went on, "Then you really are talented."

Isaac frowned, asking, "What are you talking about, Lucifer?"

"Just admit it: You aren't happy."

Isaac gave out an exasperated laugh. "Sure I'm happy."

Lucifer didn't hesitate for a moment. "No, Zack, you're not. And, to tell you the truth, fooling everyone around you is a true skill. You know, it's great for manipulating others, getting what you want. However, talented as it is, fooling yourself is something quite different; you're really holding yourself back."

"Holding myself back?" Isaac shouted.

Lucifer was unflinching, shrugging as he said, "Yes."

Isaac's eyes widened, and he tried to better express himself. "Holding *myself* back?"

Once again, Lucifer merely responded, "Yes."

"I'm not the one holding myself back! There's nothing I can do to move forward!" Isaac yelled. He then put his hand over his eyes and shook his head. Looking back up, but no longer able to look Lucifer in the eyes, Isaac continued, more softly, "I'm just trying to make the best of a bad situation."

"What do you mean?" Lucifer asked gently.

Visibly flustered, Isaac answered him, "No matter how hard I work, and no matter how hard I try, I'm never going to be anything more than a cashier."

He paused, and only then found himself able to look back at Lucifer, tears starting to well up in his eyes. "I figured I could work really hard and my boss would see my ... effort, my dedication. I figured I could get a promotion."

Isaac sighed. "I talked to my boss, and he said that he would like to give me a promotion, but God made me a cashier, so that's my job, and that will always be my job."

"But that's exactly my point," Lucifer quickly replied. "You see, by 'making the best' of this bad situation, you're only hurting yourself. Your self-deception is the big thing that's holding you back."

"What would you have me do?" Isaac immediately asked.

Lucifer said, "Well, you're not happy, right?"

Isaac nodded.

Lucifer raised his eyebrows. "Then just quit."

Isaac wrinkled his forehead. He asked, "What do you mean?"

Lucifer elaborated, "You know, quit your job. Walk up to your boss, look him square in the eye, and tell him that he can find someone else to be his cashier."

The idea seemed to confuse Isaac. "Can I ... do that?"

Lucifer replied, "Who says you can't?"

Seeing Isaac still struggling with the concept, Lucifer went on. "Your boss and God can tell you what *they* want you to do with your life, but it's still *your* life, don't forget that. You know that you can do so much more ... and so do I."

Although it was still a strange concept, Isaac was definitely considering it. Lucifer then abruptly said, "Now, how much do I owe you?"

Raphael walked through the halls of the fourteenth floor. At this time in the evening, the building was normally deserted. However, he saw that the occasional office did have lights on, angels hard at work; with the release coming faster and faster, more and more angels were staying late to finish things at the last minute.

Raphael came into the darkness of his office and flicked on the light. Turning around to get to his desk, he nearly jumped out of his skin. Lucifer was sitting on the floor, his back against his desk and his legs outstretched.

"Holy crap!" exclaimed Raphael. "What are you doing here?"

Lucifer didn't look toward Raphael. His eyes glazed over, minimal enthusiasm in his voice, he slowly answered, "Thinking ... What about you?"

It sounded as though Lucifer had absolutely no energy with which to participate in this conversation.

Raphael answered, "I wanted to get some extra work in. We do launch in three days, you know."

Lucifer lazily turned his head to Raphael, looking as though his neck hardly had the strength to keep his head up. "Oh, yeah? That's great news."

Each time Raphael saw Lucifer these days, it seemed like he was getting stranger and stranger.

"Lucifer," he said, "I don't know what's wrong with you, but I can't just sit back—"

"So I got the snowflake program up and running," Lucifer interrupted, still with a complete lack of enthusiasm.

Raphael didn't know what he was talking about. He tried to get Lucifer to clarify. "Snowflake...?"

"Yeah, you remember? The program I modified to randomly generate human personalities?"

Raphael still didn't remember anything along those lines. Seeing this, Lucifer added, "The one I stole?"

That sounded familiar. "Oh, yeah," Raphael said. "You know, you shouldn't have—"

"I didn't have any help, either," Lucifer cut him off again, still with a lack of enthusiasm. "Thanks to Michael, everyone's afraid of me."

Raphael wasn't sure that it was all Michael's fault.

Lucifer went on. "Angels don't even make eye contact anymore, but it doesn't really matter. You're the only one who knows this program's actually up and in working condition; no one else noticed. I don't have to hide anything, either. The other angels keep all the variables in their tests too highly controlled. Human personality allows for a great deal of variation, so anything they control for will be permitted; it's the fact that they put tight controls on the interactions that stops them from witnessing the truth."

Raphael looked at the phone on his desk. "So, you're saying that I need to warn Gabriel right this second."

Lucifer shrugged, slowly saying, "Whatever. You'd just be causing a panic and wasting everyone's time."

Raphael looked back at Lucifer, who sat there staring back at him. Raphael glanced at the phone once more, and then back at Lucifer.

"If you aren't lying to me about the launch date being three days away," Lucifer eventually added, "there's no way anyone can stop it. My personality program and the human physiology are intertwined, and I don't say that lightly; physiological processes themselves cause patterns of thought and behavior in humans. As such, any changes to their personality have to come from changes to their physiology, and doing so is almost impossible."

"But how can you be so sure?" Raphael asked. "How do you know that no angel will be able to change it?"

Lucifer continued his stare. "Don't misunderstand me," he said. "It's not impossible to change the humans; it's just the most difficult thing anyone can ever attempt. Electrical conduction of nerve cells is one process that allows for humans to both think and operate their organs. Protein channels are fine-tuned in structure to allow for specific ions to pass into the cell to allow for this electric conduction. Even a minute alteration to a single molecule that makes up the structure of a single protein can cause the channel to lose this specificity, no longer allowing the ion to pass through. The result would not be a useful change in function but, rather, a failure of conduction, failure of the cell, which will cause the organs to fail and, by extension, the entire human."

They sat in silence briefly.

Lucifer sighed deeply. "So, Raphael," he lazily continued, "it's not impossible to change, but it would take ... probably months, if not years or decades, to perform sufficient tests to be able to alter the physiology in a way that wouldn't outright kill every single human. It would probably be easier to start from scratch; we both know that we won't be able to do that once it's up and running, and there's definitely no time to do it before launch."

Raphael didn't know what to say. Crazy as Lucifer was sounding, Raphael knew he wasn't stupid.

"I got that other stuff going, too, the stuff I was telling you about last time," Lucifer continued to say. "You know, making humans easy to kill. That one's in the bag. To be fair, I didn't have to do much with that one. I didn't make any changes to the humans themselves; they're still remarkably resilient creatures. However—" He slowly shook his head. "The world we're placing them in is more dangerous than most angels realize. Diseases, weather, animals ... other humans. To be honest, some of the landscapes you designed are quite treacherous. Their resiliency will definitely help them out, but humans are likely to be dying all the time."

Another sigh came from Lucifer. "I did mess around with some Marketing materials as well, to make humans doubt. I made plenty of alterations to that Bible book they keep talking about; I'm sure they'll correct most of those before launch, but there's bound to be something remaining in three days' time.

"But that's not the best part. I discovered this Prayer program Marketing angels were working on, to allow humans to interact with us. What a perfect way to make them doubt our existence. The system was very straightforward and intuitive when I found out about it. Not anymore: dropped calls, corrupted data files, you name it. It will work fine for some humans, but for others, it won't even initiate. Some humans will be sure that we exist, and others will be positive that we don't. Heck, even some who initiated things properly will begin to wonder if we are actually figments of their imaginations." Lucifer turned his gaze away from Raphael and sat in silence once more.

It was now Raphael's turn to let out a sigh. "Lucifer," he said, "can I be frank with you?"

Lucifer looked at him again and nodded.

"It sounds like you're convinced that everything you told me absolutely needs to be done," Raphael went on, "but I really am having a hard time understanding. Why are you doing all of these ... horrible things?"

Lucifer focused back on the wall. He stared momentarily, but slowly turned his head back. "The thing you have to understand before asking me a question like that, Raphael," he answered, "is perspective. You can't look at what I'm doing as a simple 'right' versus 'wrong,' 'good' versus 'bad.' Is there going to be trouble and hardship in the world I'm creating? Yes. Will there be horrors the likes of which neither you nor I can comprehend? No doubt. But there will be greatness; there will be wonders the sterile world dreamt of by most angels will be incapable of providing."

Lucifer stopped speaking. He reflected on his experiences over the last few days. He considered the flood of emotions he now experienced and had long since lost the energy to contend with. He thought about how tired he was. "Remember," he finally added, "there is no 'up' or 'down' in the universe we are creating; everything is merely a frame of reference."

Raphael sat on the edge of his desk, putting a hand on his mouth, saying nothing.

Lucifer returned his eyes back to the wall. He went on with a continued lack of interest. "You know, I have to give Him credit. God, I mean. He was right; this is really happening. The project is going off without a hitch, assuming God doesn't push back the release date." He slowly shook his head once again, adding, "And you know what, Raphael? He won't."

"I have to give *you* credit as well," Raphael said.

Lucifer looked up to him, staring at Raphael, not saying a word. After some thought, Lucifer broke the silence with a simple, "Why?"

Raphael smiled. "I tried what you suggested with my program, and I'm happy with it. You were right, Lucifer."

Lucifer gave him a smile back.

Raphael went on. “You know, all this time, I wanted to ask you, since I have always wondered ... What does God look like?”

The smile left Lucifer’s face. He stared forward for some time and thought about it. Having sufficiently considered what to say, he looked back up at Raphael, merely stating, “Perfect.”

They both remained there, Raphael still worried about Lucifer but realizing that there was nothing he could do to change him back to the angel he knew and loved.

Lucifer, lowering his eyebrows, eventually spoke. “You know what, Raphael?”

“What, Lucifer?”

“I can’t be completely sure, but I think I rebelled.”

With that being said, Raphael blurted out a small laugh, the laugh thoroughly laced with sadness. He tried his best to hold back the tears that were welling up in his eyes, but he couldn’t stop them, sobbing a bit, then laughing some more.

Lucifer didn’t pay any attention to Raphael’s reaction, saying, “Where’s my promotion?”

The next day, Lucifer was busy rummaging around in his desk when he was interrupted by someone saying, “Knock, knock.”

He looked up to see a face that he’d hoped he wouldn’t have to see again: Nathaniel’s.

Nathaniel walked into the office with a smile. “Lucifer, it’s been a while. How’s everything treating you?”

Lucifer laughed under his breath, saying, “Like you care.”

Nathaniel shrugged. “I guess you’re right. Anyway, I came bearing this memo.” He whipped out a piece of paper and placed it gently on the desk in front of Lucifer.

Lucifer looked at the paper, then back up to Nathaniel. He lowered his eyebrows and said, "Well? I have a lot to do right now; just give me the gist of it."

Continuing to smile, Nathaniel smugly replied, "It would be my pleasure. It seems that you are up for a performance review. Michael is assembling all the department managers and other angels of reputable status to witness one of your presentations showing them your human models. The presentation is to be at one o'clock this afternoon in the model testing room."

"One o'clock?" Lucifer said. "Fine."

Nathaniel stepped closer. "Lucifer, I don't think you understand. Your future at this company depends on showing up to this presentation."

"Are you going to be there?" Lucifer quickly asked.

Nathaniel looked surprised at the question. "No," he replied.

"Really?" continued Lucifer. "Why? Not important enough?"

Nathaniel's face immediately reddened. He sternly added, "Just be there, Lucifer."

With that, he turned around and quickly left the office. Lucifer wasn't surprised that he wasn't given much time to prepare. Michael was probably expecting him to fly into a panic and rush his preparations in order to make him out to be a fool. Lucifer was not concerned; the big flaw in this plan was assuming he actually had to prepare. No, Lucifer had no intention of creating a special presentation for the management; he'd just use one of his test simulations. So no worry of panic ruining everything. Even so, he was fairly sure he didn't need any help in coming across the fool; given the audience and their biases toward him walking into this presentation, he could really do anything and still fail in their eyes. All he had to do was take it in stride. Plus, there was always the slim chance that just one more angel would understand. Of course, he highly doubted that would happen, considering what a bunch of narrow-minded, stuck-up prudes the other angels were.

Lucifer stood in the middle of the large white model testing room with several angels sitting nearby on folding black chairs. They watched his every move with their scrutinizing eyes. He recognized both Michael and Gabriel but no one else.

Lucifer quickly composed himself and said, “I see I have the pleasure of giving this presentation to some *very* important angels. I won’t bore you with too many details—”

“Get on with it, Lucifer,” Michael interrupted him.

Lucifer lowered his eyebrows and slowly finished his thought. “As I was saying ... I’ll get right into it.” He glared at Michael, receiving a stern look back. Lucifer spoke up. “Run program P-A-C dot two.”

Immediately, a couch appeared beside Lucifer. On it, two male humans and one female human sat watching the television that also appeared across from them. Despite static being the only thing appearing on the television screen, all three humans focused their attention upon it. Between the humans and the television was a small table with empty beer bottles strewn all about. Lucifer stepped off to the side and observed the interaction carefully. The other angels fixed their eyes upon the humans, some of the angels jotting down notes upon their clipboards.

They watched as the female’s eyes began to grow heavy and slowly closed. Her head came to rest on the shoulder of the male sitting beside her. As she fell asleep, the eyes of the male whose shoulder she had laid her head upon widened. He looked at her, just moving his eyes. His head still motionless, his eyes went to the other male, who was still focused on the static. He returned his gaze to the woman and slowly reached one of his hands over, gently touching her breast. His eyes widened even more as he did so; he observed as her nipple gradually hardened to his touch.

He found it harder and harder to resist. He reached around her with one arm and grasped both breasts firmly in his hands, massaging them sensually. She gave a sleepy moan, shifting her weight slightly, but did not awaken, obviously sleeping deeply as a result of her intoxication.

At this time, the other male casually glanced over. It took him a few seconds to register what was happening, but once he realized, he immediately whispered, "Andrew, what do you think you're doing?"

Andrew looked back at the other male, still groping the female. He whispered, "Butt out, Paul. You need to mind your own business."

Paul shook his head, quietly adding, "No, man. That's so wrong."

Andrew raised his eyebrows and smiled back at Paul, saying, "But she likes it."

"How would you know?" Paul still tried to whisper but was failing at his attempt to remain quiet. "She's fucking asleep!"

Andrew, still whispering, retorted, "Shut up, man. Besides, she wouldn't have dressed like that if she didn't want some action." He smiled again, continuing, "She's not even wearing a bra."

Paul stood up. His tone became very serious and much louder. "You'd better stop it, Andrew."

"Or what are you going to do?" Andrew asked, one of his hands slowly moving down her stomach to the top of her pants. His hand made its way down to her fly, and he began undoing the button.

Paul couldn't stand to watch him any longer. He grabbed Andrew by the collar of his shirt with both hands and pulled him up to his feet. In doing so, he caused the female to flop over on the couch, and it looked as though the commotion was beginning to wake her.

Andrew yelled, "Leave me alone, dude. Let a guy have some fucking fun!"

With that, Andrew forcibly removed Paul's hands from his collar. Spinning around, Andrew shoved Paul in the chest very hard, causing Paul to take a step back. Almost immediately, Paul sprang back and hit Andrew square in the jaw with everything he had. Andrew wobbled slightly from the blow, and Paul took the opportunity to bring Andrew down with a tackle. As they went down to the ground hard, Andrew ate another punch to the face.

Michael jumped up to his feet, tossing his clipboard and yelling, "Freeze models!"

With that, the humans froze in place, the female only now starting to realize what was unfolding around her, drowsy as she was. Paul was stuck where he was, on top of Andrew, winding up for another punch with unbridled rage in his eyes. Andrew, lying on the ground with his eyes closed, grimaced in pain as he spit up some blood, which was suspended in the air immediately above his face.

A smash was heard as Michael's clipboard landed. Lucifer turned to him, a disappointed look on his face.

"Why'd you do that? It was just starting to get good!"

"I can't watch this anymore!" Michael shouted.

Lucifer smiled, pointing at the humans but still facing Michael as he spoke. "Interestingly, I have never seen Paul attack Andrew so aggressively before. He usually gets too intimidated and gives up. It was beautiful."

Michael clearly didn't see it the same way. "How can you say that? You have a serious problem! That was horrid!"

Lucifer looked to the other angels and saw from the disgust on their faces that they agreed with Michael.

He sighed. Looking back to Michael, Lucifer said, "If you thought *that* was horrible, you should have seen what happened last time."

Words failed Michael. All he could do was stand there, dumbfounded.

Lucifer continued, "Let's just say that Paul was very ... weak."

Gabriel and Michael sat across from God in His office. The other managers all vividly expressed their concerns pertaining to Lucifer, and they made their opinions on what should be done with him very clear, but because he was an employee under the Research and Development department, it was decided that Gabriel should be the one to come to a decision with God. However, Michael, knowing that Gabriel was a big softy, insisted on tagging along to ensure they didn't go too easy on Lucifer. Both angels waited for Him to address them before speaking.

God sat there in silence for some time, thinking long and hard about the matter at hand. Eventually, He spoke. "So, all the department managers are concerned that Lucifer needs to be dealt with?"

"Without a doubt," Michael immediately piped up. "If he's left to his own devices, there's no telling what he's capable of."

"How can we be sure that he hasn't already caused a number of problems with the project?" asked God.

Michael smiled. "There's no need to worry about that. I've been on top of the situation since the first complaint came in, and everyone I talked to assured me that they did not give him a shred of aid in his quest to destroy everything we have been working toward. The launch will not be compromised."

"Good," God said. He looked to Gabriel. "And I understand that these numerous issues that have been brought up came to the fore during his performance review?"

Michael answered for Gabriel. "Absolutely. More horrendous things I have never seen. Deal with him now so we don't have to continually babysit, so we can focus on the future."

Once Michael finished what he had to say, God did not continue speaking. He just kept staring at Gabriel, who would not look at the Lord.

God eventually spoke to Gabriel again, "Gabriel, have you nothing to add to this discussion? We *are* speaking of the future of an employee from your department."

Gabriel looked up, first to God and then to Michael. With his eyes, Michael coaxed Gabriel on.

Gabriel looked back at God, saying, "I don't know."

Michael continued looking at him, now with bewilderment. God merely sat, waiting for Gabriel to continue. He did.

"I agree with Michael. We can't just ignore it when an angel seems to be ... actively losing his mind. Right now, he's a loose cannon. If he hasn't done anything yet, as Michael says, I'm not worried about the release date, but we need to ensure he can't get in there and ruin anything once it's up and running. And I don't think I'll be able to trust him for future projects, so I'm going to have to say ... get rid of him."

Michael smiled. "Okay. Well, let's not spare a second, then."

"Wait," God said. Still looking only at Gabriel, He went on. "There's more to it."

Gabriel looked up to God.

God continued, "There's something that isn't sitting well with you, isn't that right, Gabriel?"

Gabriel stared into God's eyes, "Well, yes. It's just that ... the whole time I was watching the demonstration ... Michael is right. It was despicable, and I could see the look in Lucifer's eyes; he was enjoying the whole display. But there was something he said afterwards that really got me thinking. He said that something different happened last time. It sounded to me like the interaction changes each time he sees it."

"You can't trust anything that angel has to say," interjected Michael.

At that time, God raised His hand, and Michael took that to signal him to stop speaking. As such, he obeyed.

God, not taking His eyes off Gabriel, said, "Go on."

Gabriel did as God ordered. "Every single interaction I've ever seen in the model testing room was just a scripted one. The programmer merely made some humans, stuck them together, and made them speak. This was the only time I believe I truly saw ... life."

God nodded. "So, what do you propose we do?"

Gabriel put his hand up to his mouth, and looked away from God, considering it deeply. "I don't know."

All three sat in silence for a moment.

Gabriel looked back at God. "If we could only postpone the launch, we could see if we could fix his program ... We could make it much more ... bearable."

"Impossible," God replied. "The launch cannot be delayed. And, I assure you, Gabriel, the project is to My liking, without us altering Lucifer's program and utilizing it."

Gabriel sighed, "I suppose you're right."

God looked at Michael and back at Gabriel. "So, what now?"

Gabriel asked, "What do You mean?"

God elaborated on His question. "What, now, should I do with Lucifer?"

Michael and Gabriel looked at each other. Michael spoke up.

"Get rid of him. There's no way we can keep him on."

God looked to Gabriel.

Gabriel gave another deep sigh. "I suppose Michael's right. Like I said, I don't think I could ever trust him to work on another project. I just wish he didn't ... go insane. He really was quite brilliant."

God nodded. "If that is how each of you feels, it shall be done."

Lucifer and Raphael sat alone in their office. Raphael quietly scribbled on his papers. At this point, he was more or less ready for the launch, but he was tying up loose ends and finalizing everything. Lucifer sat at his desk, which was completely bare, and just stared at the wall, awaiting his fate.

Raphael said, "Hey, once we launch, want to head out to the Pearly Gates? I'm buying."

Lucifer simply stated, "No, thanks."

That was not the response Raphael was expecting. He turned around to look at Lucifer. "What do you mean by that? We have a lot to celebrate. You seem to have everything in order, so it's not as if you're going to be all stressed out right afterwards anyway. Come on."

"I just don't think I'm going to be in a position to celebrate by your side, Raphael."

Raphael became very concerned, "Lucifer ... what are you talking about?"

Still staring at the wall, Lucifer answered, "You'll find out soon enough."

They each heard a low rumbling. Raphael looked all around, but he could not locate the source of the sound.

Lucifer glanced down at his watch and added, "Much sooner than I'd expected."

The rumbling grew, as though the cause of it was getting closer. The office began to shake. Raphael became very frightened; the shaking worsened to the point that Raphael's pile of notes fell from his desk onto the floor. He grabbed his desk tightly. Suddenly, the ceiling in the middle of the room began to split apart, wind building up as it did so. Very quickly, the hole being created widened until it crumbled away, the pieces flying into the air rather than falling to the ground, until the office was no longer covered. The wind became so strong that papers flew all around them in a whirlwind. Lucifer got to his feet and moved to the center of the clearing, looking up. Raphael looked up as well, but cautiously made his way to one of the walls. They both watched as the same thing happened to the ceiling for the floor above them, and the ceiling above that, and so on, faster and faster, until it was so high up the building that they could not be sure of what floor it reached.

Pages still flying all around them, the rumbling stopped. Lucifer remained where he was, looking up. Raphael carefully stepped out a bit to see if anything was happening. At that very moment, something large came crashing down and landed in their office with a loud thud. It was a large being, at least twenty feet tall with arms and legs as thick as tree trunks. Both angels didn't know why, but, deep in their hearts, they both innately knew it was God. He did not appear hurt when landing, but He came down with such a deafening impact that craters were formed around His feet. Raphael stood behind God in awe; God stood looking down at Lucifer, who did not appear at all surprised.

In a loud booming voice, God said, "For your attempted rebellion against your Master and your continued insolence toward Me and all angelic beings, I, the Lord, the Creator, hereby banish you, Lucifer, to the fiery pits of Hell for all eternity, never to return."

With that, the Lord held up His hand. Lucifer smiled. In God's hand, swirling darkness was slowly aggregating, growing bigger and bigger until it became larger than Lucifer himself. God cast the ball of darkness at Lucifer. To Raphael's horror, it collided with Lucifer, consuming him entirely with a flash of light.

The wind began to die down. God remained where He was, but Lucifer was no more.

Raphael moved closer to the Lord, yelling, "What have You done?"

But it made no difference to God. He did not give Raphael any acknowledgement, and immediately shot up into the sky. Almost as quickly as He'd left, the ceiling reassembled itself. The wind stopped; the only evidence of God's arrival that remained, aside from the papers blown all over the floor, were the two large craters in the middle of the room.

Chapter 15

Revelations

Eve emerged from the flowing brook in naked splendor. She stepped out of the warm water and walked, dripping, onto the riverbank, the air as warm as the water she came out of. Feeling hunger, she walked past the lush bushes to a low-hanging banana in a nearby tree and easily pulled it off the branch. She began to peel it, but stopped when she heard someone speak.

"A lovely day, is it not?"

Looking up, Eve saw that it was a serpent hanging from one of the branches who had beckoned to her.

"It always is here," was her reply.

"But of course."

The serpent gave her a disappointed look, and she grew concerned.

"What seems to be the trouble?" she asked.

"It just pains me to see your delicate lips waste their time with that ordinary banana." He pointed with the end of his tail into the foliage. "In there is much more suitable sustenance to please a beauty such as yourself."

"You speak madness, serpent," Eve responded. "The farther away from here I wander, the less flavorful the fruits become."

"Ah, but you have been deceived," the serpent went on.

He could see her eyes widen as her intrigue grew, but Eve merely stated, "I know not what you speak of."

He slithered closer to her, elaborating on what he had said. "A common tactic for hiding that which one does not want found. Believe me. I would not lie to you. Go into the trees, and there, deep within those that you find to be undesirable, will be fruits unlike anything in your wildest fantasies."

Eve looked into the trees and then back to the serpent. He could see from the look on her face that she currently was skeptical, but his idea was successfully planted, and it would be only a matter of time before her perfect life gave way for further curiosity and the idea blossomed.

Iguana Books

iguanabooks.com

If you enjoyed *Lucifer*...

Look for other books coming soon from Iguana Books! Subscribe to our blog for updates as they happen.

iguanabooks.com/blog/

You can also learn more about Alexander Kosoris and his upcoming work on his blog.

kosoris.com/blog

If you're a writer...

Iguana Books is always looking for great new writers, in every genre. We produce primarily ebooks but, as you can see, we do the occasional print book as well. Visit us at iguanabooks.com to see what Iguana Books has to offer both emerging and established authors.

iguanabooks.com/publishing-with-iguana/

If you're looking for another good book ...

All Iguana Books books are available on our website. We pride ourselves on making sure that every Iguana book is a great read.

iguanabooks.com/bookstore/

Visit our bookstore today and support your favourite author.